STUDIES IN
JAIMINI ASTROLOGY

BANGALORE VENKATA RAMAN

MOTILAL BANARSIDASS PUBLISHERS
PRIVATE LIMITED • DELHI

5th Reprint : Delhi. 2018
Fifth Revised Edition : Bangalore, 1986

ISBN: 978-81-208-1397-7

MOTILAL BANARSIDASS
41 U.A. Bungalow Road, Jawahar Nagar, Delhi 110 007
1 B, Jyoti Studio Compound, Kennedy Bridge, Nana Chowk, Mumbai 400 007
203 Royapettah High Road, Mylapore, Chennai 600 004
236, 9th Main III Block, Jayanagar, Bengaluru 560 011
8 Camac Street, Kolkata 700 017
Ashok Rajpath, Patna 800 004
Chowk, Varanasi 221 001

Printed in India
by RP Jain at NAB Printing Unit,
A-44, Naraina Industrial Area, Phase I, New Delhi–110028
and published by JP Jain for Motilal Banarsidass Publishers (P) Ltd,
41 U.A. Bungalow Road, Jawahar Nagar, Delhi-110007

Preface

My interest in Jaimini was aroused over 20 years ago when I was yet a college student by a Kerala Brahmin astrologer who was practising near my residence. What struck me most was his admirable analysis of the fourth house in my horoscope, according to Jaimini, supported by eloquent quotations from the SUTRAS. He gave me to understand then that the 3rd and 4th Adhyayas had been lost and that they were not to be found either in print or in manuscript form anywhere. By about 1936 an advocate friend of mine presented me with a copy of **Jaimini Sutras** in Kannada script which also contained the original sutras of the 3rd and 4th Adhyayas. The Kerala astrologer was kind enough to interpret the 3rd and 4th Adhyayas for my benefit and I am grateful to him for this help. Subsequently he shifted his office and I lost touch with him. Since then my interest in Jaimini began to grow and I gathered valuable information through my discussions with Pandits who used to visit my grandfather late Prof. B. Suryanarain Rao.

I have with me a number of versions of Jaimini in Devanagari, Kannada and Telugu scripts—most of them containing Neelakanta's commentaries. And the present work which I have the pleasure to place before the educated public is mainly based upon my "STUDIES" done during the last fifteen years. Owing probably to the dearth of books dealing clearly with the principles, and of scholars who have specialised in this particular branch of astrological knowledge, Jaimini's methods have not been popular. Consequently it is not possible to say with what degree of success the principles given by Jaimini could be applied to practical horoscopes. But there is no doubt whatsoever that when once the technique of prediction as given by Jaimini has been clearly grasped, considerable accuracy could be aimed at.

In these STUDIES I have merely endeavoured to make available in compact and simple form the leading facts or concepts of Jaimini's principles. Certain aspects of Jaimini such as Dasas, Ayurdaya, etc., which have hitherto remained obscure, have been dealt with exhaustively and their significance shown. I do not claim originality. But I claim to be the first in India to have given an exposition of Jaimini in English with suitable illustrations.

It should be pointed out in conclusion that if this work were to stimulate a more detailed study of Jaimini, my labours will have been amply rewarded.

Bangalore,
Vijayadasami, *B. V. RAMAN.*
20th October, 1950.

Preface to the Fifth Edition

It is with great pleasure that I present herewith the fifth edition of my STUDIES IN JAIMINI ASTROLOGY.

The fourth edition went out of print a couple of years ago and the bringing out of the fifth edition had to be delayed due to my other preoccupations.

This edition has been revised and typographical and other errors have been eliminated.

Jaimini has certain special features especially bearing on longevity and Dasa interpretation furnishing fresh material for the research-minded. The information given in this book has been based on all the four chapters of the SUTRAS and has been tested by me on several horoscopes.

In fact as early as 1944, even before I brought out the first edition, I had made predictions based on Jaimini on the horoscopes of Hitler and Mussolini which were remarkably fulfilled.

I am thankful to Mr. G. K. Ananthram for having brought out this edition attractively.

I hope that astrological savants will welcome this new edition as they have welcomed all my other books.

Bangalore
29-11-1986

B. V. RAMAN

Contents

ARTICLE PAGE

Chapter—II (Contd.)

Chapter III—Aspects and Argalas

CHAPTER 1

Preliminary Observations

1. Jaimini and Parasari

The Jaimini system of Astrology upon which these *Studies* are based marks a definite departure from the canons of Parasari, or the general system of Astrology now in vogue throughout India. It cannot be maintained however that Jaimini and Parasari are at complete variance from each other or they are two distinct systems. On the contrary, it seems reasonable to suppose, that Jaimini is merely an offshoot of the general scheme of the astrological science propounded by Parasara, for in the works of Parasara and Vriddhayavana, frequent references are to be found to the specific and distinct methodology employed by Jaimini. For instance, in Adhyaya 1, Pada 1, Sutra 5, Jaimini says that planets in the 4th, 2nd and 11th from an aspecting body cause Argalas. Parasara simply confirms this in his *Hora Sastra*. Similarly in the matter of counteraction of Argalas, determination of Karakas, Arudha Lagna, results of Karakamsa, determination of longevity, etc., it looks as though Parasara and Vriddhayavana confirm Jaimini. This might tempt one to conclude that Parasara and Vriddhayavana must probably have been later writers. Such a conclusion would be unwarranted because Parasara, being the progenitor of Vyasa, could not have lived after Jaimini. The source of all astrological knowledge in India is undoubtedly Parasara. Jaimini must have picked up certain aspects of Parasari and given them a new orientation consistent with his own genius, and thus developed almost a new system which did not become popular with the majority of the astrological savants because of the fact, the principles were presented in the shape of *Sutras* or aphorisms which are always capable of a variety of interpretations. Subsequently, savants like Neelakantha and Premanidhi have tried to elucidate or explain these Sutras by way of valuable commentaries, thus facilitating their easy comprehension by the rank and file of scholars.

The Jaimini system has its own distinctive features. The introduction of Karakas, the peculiar methods of determination of longevity, the simplicity with which the strength of planets is reckoned, the apparently complicated processes involved in the working of the various types of Dasas, the emphasis laid on the conception horoscope, the distinction attached to Arudha Lagna and the great importance given to the Karakamsa, and its bearing on the determination of one's livelihood, invest the whole system with a certain amount of uniqueness and originality, that it is no wonder it came to be looked upon as a separate branch of astrological knowledge, though the Jaimini system is doubtless a part and parcel of Parasari.

2. Differences

We can see quite a number of so-called 'differences' between Parasari and Jaimini. In the first place, Rasis in Jaimini are synonymous with Bhavas or Houses, while in Parasari, the distinction between signs (Rasis) and Houses (Bhavas) is well marked. Aspects are not based upon mutual distances of planets. The Karakas are constants in Parasari while in Jaimini they are variable. The Shadbala strengths considered in Parasari involve elaborate calculations while Jaimini dispenses with cumbersome calculations and suggests simple rules for evaluating planetary strengths. In the determination of Ayurdaya (longevity), in the description of various Yogas, in the mode of reckoning and interpretation of Dasas and in fact in almost every respect, fresh and entirely novel ground has been covered by the Maharshi. It looks as though some kind of special ability is required on the part of one who wants to understand Jaimini correctly.

3. Jaimini's Abstruseness

The Sage is often abstruse in some of his observations. For instance, reference is made to a number of Dasas. Under what specific conditions, the different Dasas are to be employed ? The reader is left to guess for himself. And as far as I could see, no clue is given anywhere in all the four Adhyayas of the Sutras. I am not unaware of the suggestions to be found here and there (*vide* for example A. 2, P. 4, Su. 1) that for knowing the results of a particular Bhava, a certain type of Dasa is to be preferred. But the instructions do not appear to be clear. There have been attempts on the part of some recent writers to unnecessarily strain the Sutras with a view to discovering the clue. But I am afraid such an approach is not the right one. My discussions with a number of scholars and a perusal of the extant literature on this particular branch of astrology lead me to the conclusion that the Sage generally favours Charadasa (Art. 75 *et. seq.*) not only for determining longevity but also for predicting important events to happen during the life of a person. It is for readers to decide for themselves the Dasa which would give the most satisfactory results in actual practice. Wherever I have found a certain sutra tough, vague or capable of a two-fold interpretation (probably because of my own incapacity or inability to understand the true import of the sutra properly) I have invariably had recourse to the explanations of Parasara or Vriddhayavana or collateral literature dealing with the technique of Jaimini.

As the name of the book implies, these *Studies* are intended to bring to the attention of the educated public, a summary of the principles of Jaimini, as understood by me.

In Adhyaya III, Pada 2, the Sage has given a number of combinations bearing upon the different Bhavas but applicable to Adhana Lagna, but in these *Studies* I have suggested their application to the birth horoscope, because, in almost all classical works, whenever a Prasna Lagna or Adhana Lagna is mentioned, Janma Lagna is invariably implied.

4. Standard Horoscope

For purposes of illustrating the mathematical aspect of Jaimini Astrology, I propose to consider the nativity of a person born on 12-2-1856 A.D. at 12-21 p.m. corresponding to Gh. 14-30 after sunrise, Long. 84° E; Lat. 18° N. The following are the planetary longitudes and the Rasi and Navamsa Diagrams.

Planet	*Rasi*	*Degree*	*Minute*
Ravi	Kumbha	1	12
Chandra	Mesha	18	29
Kuja	Thula	0	53
Budha	Kumbha	8	27
Guru	Kumbha	21	38
Sukra	Dhanus	20	33
Sani	Mithuna	3	20
Rahu	Mesha	6	9
Ketu	Thula	6	9
Lagna	Vrishabha	13	9

	Rahu Chandra *Upapada*	Lagna	Sani
Ravi Budha Guru (A.K.)	RASI		*Aru- dha Gha- tika Lagna*
Sukra *Var- nada Lagna*		*Hora Lagna* Kuja Ketu	A. 7

	Kara- kamsa Lagna Guru	Rahu *Hora Lagna*	
	NAVAMSA		
Budha	Ketu *Ghatika Lagna*	Ravi Sani Sukra Kuja	Chan- dra

CHAPTER II

The Essentials Explained

5. The Karakas

Each planet is supposed to be the Karaka or indicator of certain events in life. The functions of a Karaka are similar to those of the Bhava or house. Karakas play an important part in horoscope analysis.

6. Natural Karakas

According to Parasari, the Karaka planets are all constant irrespective of their horoscopic positions. The following are the main Karakas :—

Planet	*Karaka*
Ravi or the Sun	Father
Chandra or the Moon	Mother
Kuja or Mars	Brothers
Budha or Mercury	Profession
Guru or Jupiter	Children
Sukra or Venus	Wife or husband
Sani or Saturn	Longevity
Rahu or Caput	Maternal Relations
Ketu or Cauda	Paternal Relations

Karakas become important factors especially in measuring Gochara or transit results. Even when a certain Bhava is weak, the event signified by the Bhava could be said to prosper provided the appropriate Karaka is strong.

7. Karakas in Jaimini

Karakas according to the scheme of Jaimini vary with regard to each horoscope. This feature is of great significance. Any planet can acquire any karakatwa or lordship, as the basis for determining the karaka is merely the longitude of a planet reckoned from the beginning of the sign concerned. There are 7 main karakas in Jaimini, *viz.*, (1) Atma, (2) Amatya, (3) Bhratru, (4) Matru, (5) Putra, (6) Gnathi and (7) Dara.

8. Atmakaraka

The chief or prime-lord or indicator is all important. The planet having the highest longitude in a sign becomes the Atmakaraka. The strength or weakness of the Atmakaraka seems to reflect the general strength or weakness of the entire horoscope, so that the position of the Atmakaraka is very important. The natural Atmakaraka is however Ravi or the Sun.

9. Amatyakaraka

The next in importance is the Amatyakaraka. Devoid of the signs, the planet who gets the next greatest number of degrees becomes the Amatyakaraka or the sub-lord. There is no naisargika (natural or permanent) Amatyakaraka but we may assume Budha or Mercury to be as such.

10. Bhratrukaraka

The planet whose longitude is next to that of Amatyakaraka becomes the lord of brothers. All events pertaining to brothers and sisters have to be read from Bhratrukaraka. Kuja or Mars is the naisargikakaraka for brothers.

11. Matrukaraka

The lord of mother is the planet that gets the next highest number of degrees in a sign. Chandra or the Moon is however the natural karaka of mother.

12. Putrakaraka

The lord of children is the planet that gets the next largest number of degrees devoid of the signs. The natural or naisargika indicator of this horoscopic function is Guru or Jupiter.

13. Gnathikaraka

The planet whose longitude is less than that of Putrakaraka becomes the lord of relations. The natural karaka or indicator for *Gnathis* or cousins and relations is Kuja or Mars.

14. Darakaraka

The lord of wife (or husband) is the one whose longitude is least. The natural Dara or Kalatrakaraka is Sukra or Venus.

15. Determination of Karakas

Summarising the above, convert the longitudes of the 7 planets into signs, degrees, minutes and seconds. Reject the signs and considering the degrees, minutes, etc., tabulate the positions of planets in the descending order of their number of degrees. The planet whose longitude is the highest becomes the Atmakaraka. The rest follow according to the above order. It will be seen that the order of Karakas is exactly similar to the order of Bhavas from the first to seven except that while the second Karaka is styled Amatya, the second Bhava refers to finance or Dhana.

16. Exceptions

There are certain exceptions to the general rule governing Karaka determination. Sometimes two or more planets may occupy the same degree of longitude, so that they may have to share the same lordship. A contingency like this rarely occurs but it cannot be entirely ruled out. Under such an exceptional circumstance, when two or three planets have to share the same *lordship*, a few lordships become vacant and these have to be filled up by Rahu and the other natural Karakas. Supposing Ravi is the Bhratrukaraka and Chandra and Kuja have the same longitude. Then all the three planets become Bhratrukarakas. This means that the Karakatwas, which Chandra and Kuja should have got, fall vacant. If in the above instance, Matru and Putrakarakas become vacant on account of Chandra and Kuja sharing Ravi's functions, then Rahu becomes Matrukaraka and Guru, the natural lord of children, becomes the Putrakaraka. Such a development hardly occurs. Rahu could be a candidate for a lordship only when two or more planets have equal longitudes. Otherwise he is not eligible. The 2nd part of the Sutra (Saptanamashtanamva) in which Jaimini defines karaka determination means "seven planets from Sun to Saturn or eight planets from Sun to Rahu". Commentators have differently interpreted this part of the Sutra. According to some, there are 8 karakas (including Pitrukaraka which has been omitted in some versions of Jaimini) in which case the Sun to Rahu become Atma and other karakas according to their longitude (Rahu's longitude being measured from the last part of the sign) while according to others there are only seven karakas—Sun to Saturn Pitrukaraka omitted) and Rahu supplies the gap formed when two or more planets hold the same longitude. The latter view appears more reasonable as it has the support of Parasara.* Rahu can be taken as the 8th planet only when two or more planets have the same longitude.

Example 1

Determine the Karakas in the Standard Horoscope.

Tabulating the positions of planets according to the descending order of their degrees, we have :—

Planet		*Rasi*		*Degree*	*Minute*
Guru or Jupiter	...	Kumbha	(♒)	21	38
Sukra or Venus	...	Dhanus	(♐)	20	33
Chandra or Moon	...	Mesha	(♈)	18	29
Budha or Mercury	...	Kumbha	(♒)	8	27
Rahu or Caput	...	Mesha	(♈)	6	9
Ketu or Cauda	...	Thula	(♎)	6	9
Sani or Saturn	...	Mithuna	(♓)	3	20
Ravi or Sun	...	Kumbha	(♒)	1	12
Kuja or Mars	...	Thula	(♎)	0	53

Since Jupiter has the highest longitude, he becomes the Atmakaraka. The next highest is secured by Venus who becomes Amatyakaraka. The other planets similarly considered get the following functions :—

Karaka		*Lord*	
Atmakaraka	...	Guru	(♃)
Amatyakaraka	...	Sukra	(♀)
Bhratrukaraka	...	Chandra	(☽)
Matrukaraka	...	Budha	(☿)

* Ravyadi Sani Paryanta bhavanti saptakarakaha ;
Amsaih samyam grahaih dwou cha Rahum tangunayodwijaha,

Karaka			*Lord*
Putrakaraka	...	Sani	(♄)
Gnathikaraka	...	Ravi	(☉)
Darakaraka	...	Kuja	(♂)

17. Minor Karakas

The following allocation of some minor Karakas, suggested by Jaimini's commentators, would be helpful in predicting events correctly. (1) *Mars*—Sisters, younger brothers, step-mother and brothers-in-law. (2) *Mercury*—Maternal uncles, maternal aunts. (3) *Jupiter*—Paternal grandfather and grandmother. (4) *Venus*—Wife's parents, maternal grandparents.

18. Different Kinds of Lagnas

For making predictions, reference is made to different kinds of Ascendants. They are :—(1) Arudha Lagna, (2) Bhava Lagna, (3) Hora Lagna, (4) Varnada Lagna, (5) Ghatika Lagna and (6) Nisheka Lagna.

19. Arudha Lagna

Count as many signs from birth lord as the lord is removed from the Ascendant. This will give Arudha or Pada Lagna. Suppose Aquarius or Kumbha is the Lagna and the lord is in Taurus, the 4th from Lagna. Then the 4th from Taurus, *viz.*, Simha would be the Arudha Lagna.

Example 2

Determine the Arudha Lagna in the Standard Horoscope.

Lagna is Taurus. Lord of Lagna Venus is in Sagittarius, 8th from Lagna. Therefore the 8th from Sagittarius, *viz.*, Cancer is the Arudha Lagna.

20. Hora Lagna*

Divide the time of birth in ghatis (from sunrise) by 2.5. The quotient *plus* one counted from the Sun or Lagna according as the Janma Lagna is odd or even, represents the Hora Lagna. The remainder reduced to degrees gives the exact longitude of Hora Lagna.

Example 3

Find out the Hora Lagna in the Standard Horoscope.

Lagna is Taurus—an even sign.

Time of birth is 14.5 ghatis after sunrise.

Dividing the birth time by 2.5, $\frac{14.5}{2.5}$ we get 5 as quotient and 0.8 as remainder.

Since Lagna is even, the 6th (5+1) from Lagna, *viz.*, Thula becomes the Hora Lagna. The remainder, *viz.*, 0.8 multiplied by 30 gives 24°.

∴ Hora Lagna = Thula 24°.

---

* The methods suggested for calculating Hora Lagna, Bhava Lagna, etc., appear to be mathematically unsound unless the exact longitude of the Lagna is not desired. For Hora Lagna, each hora or 2.5 ghatis being equal to 1 sign or 30°, each ghati would be equivalent to 12°. Mathematically, Birth Ghatis (after sunrise) into 12, counted from the (exact longitude of) Sun or that of Lagna according as Lagna is odd or even should give the Hora Lagna. In Expmple 3, the Hora Lagna would be 14.5 × 12 = 174°.0 away from the Birth Lagna. Hence mathematically the exact position of Hora Lagna would be 43° 9′ + 174° = 217° 9′ = Scorpio 7° 9′. Actually, however, as we are asked to count from the sign of Lagna (*i.e.*, from the 1st degree of the Lagna Rasi), we get 30 + 174 = 204° = Thula 24°.

21. Bhava Lagna*

This is the sign arrived at by counting $n+1$ places from the Sun or Janma Lagna according as the Janma Lagna is odd or even. n is an integral quotient arrived at by dividing the birth ghatis by 5. The remainder reduced to degrees gives the exact longitude of Bhava Lagna.

Example 4

Find the Bhava Lagna in the Standard Horoscope.

Janma Lagna is Taurus, an even sign.

Birth Ghatis = 14.5.

$$\therefore n = \frac{14.5}{5} = 2.9 = \text{Quotient} = 2\ ;\ \text{Remainder} = 0.9$$

$\because$ Janma Lagna is an even sign, Bhava Lagna is the 3rd ($n+1$) from Janma Lagna, *viz.*, Cancer.

Multiplying the remainder by 30, we get 27° as the exact longitude of Bhava Lagna.

$\therefore$ Bhava Lagna = Cancer 27°.

22. Varnada Lagna

If the Janma Lagna is an odd sign, count clockwise from Mesha to Janma Lagna. If the Janma Lagna is even, count anti-clockwise from Pisces to Janma Lagna. Call this *a*. Similarly according as Hora Lagna is odd or even, count from Mesha (clockwise) or Meena (anti-clockwise) to Hora Lagna. Call this *b*. If both Janma and Hora Lagnas are odd or both even, then take the sum of *a* and *b*. If one is odd and the other is even, take the difference

* Mathematically Bhava Lagna is obtained by adding birth ghatis from sunrise × 6, to longitude of Lagna or the Sun according as the Lagna is odd or even. In the Standard Horoscope, birth ghatis × 6 = 87°. This added to 43° 9′ (longitude of Lagna) gives 130° 9′ = Leo 10° 9′ as Bhava Lagna. Actually, however, 87° is added to the 1st degree of Lagna : (30 + 87) = 117 = Cancer 27°.

between *a* and *b*, call this *c*. Expunge multiples of 12 and Varnada Lagna is the Rasi arrived at by counting *c* from Mesha (direct) or Meena (reverse) according as the Janma Lagna is odd or even.

Example 5

Determine the Varnada Lagna in the Standard Horoscope.

Janma Lagna is Taurus—an even sign.

Hora Lagna is Libra—an odd sign.

$\therefore$ $a=11$ (counting in the reverse order from Pisces to Janma Lagna).

$b=7$ (counting in the direct order from Mesha to Hora Lagna).

$\because$ Janma Lagna is even and Hora Lagna is odd

$a-b=c$ (after expunging multiples of 12)

$11-7=4$ (after expunging multiples of 12)

As Janma Lagna is an even sign, the 4th from Pisces, counted in the reverse order, *viz.*, Dhanus is the Varnada Lagna.

23. Varnadas for other Rasis

Just as we calculated Varnada for Lagna, we can calculate Varnadas for all the other 11 Bhavas by treating the appropriate Rasi as Lagna. If Varnada for 2nd Rasi is required, then treat it as Lagna and the 2nd Rasi from Hora Lagna takes the place of Hora Lagna for purposes of Varnada calculation. If Varnada for the 3rd is required, the 3rd from Hora Lagna takes the place of Hora Lagna. Similarly other Bhavas must be dealt with.

Example 6

Calculate the Varnada for the 2nd Rasi in the Standard Horoscope.

The 2nd Rasi is Gemini—an odd sign.
The 2nd from Hora Lagna is Vrischikha—an even sign.
∴ $a = 3$ (counting in the direct order from Meena to Mithuna, the second Rasi).
$b = 5$ (counting in the reverse order from Meena to Vrischika, 2nd from Hora Lagna).
∴ 2nd Rasi is odd and the 2nd from Hora even.
Take the difference between a and $b = 5 - 3 = 2$.

As the 2nd Rasi is an odd sign, the 2nd from Mesha counted in the direct order, *viz.*, Vrishabha is the Varnada of the 2nd Rasi. Varnadas for different Rasis would be required for calculating Varnada Dasa (see art. 95).

24. Ghatika Lagna*

Divide the birth ghatis by 12, reject the quotient and the integral part of the remainder (n) plus 1 counted from Janma Lagna gives the Ghatika Lagna. The fractional part of the remainder reduced to degree gives the exact longitude.

Example 7

Find the Ghatika Lagna in the Standard Horoscope.
Janma Lagna is Taurus.
Birth time in Ghatis = 14.5

* Mathematically, each Ghati becomes equivalent to 30°. Hence Ghatika Lagna can be obtained by multiplying birth ghatis from sunrise by 30 and adding the product to the longitude of Lagna. In the Standard Horoscope, the Ghatika Lagna according to strictly mathematical rules would be :

478° 9′ = 118° 9′ = Cancer 28° 9′
= 435° + 43° 9′ = (14.5 × 30) 43° 9′

Actually, however, we are asked to add Birth ghatis × 30 to the first point of Lagna. This gives Gnatika Lagna as 15° of Cancer.

Dividing the birth ghatis by 12,

we get $\frac{145}{12} = 2.5$ (remainder).

The integral part is 2; fractional part 0.5; Ghatika Lagna is the Rasi arrived at by counting $n+1=(2+1)$, *i.e.*, 3rd from Janma Lagna, *viz.*, Kataka. The remainder part, *viz.*, 0.5 reduced to degrees gives 15°.

∴ Ghatika Lagna = Cancer 15°.

25. Nisheka or Adhana Lagna

This is the sign rising at the time of conception. There is a widespread belief current amongst some modern astrological students who always look to the West for astrological inspiration that Prenatal astrology was developed in the West. Such a misconception is partly due to ignorance and partly to prepossession that a theory involving astronomico-biological correlations could not have been developed by the ancients. To the utter disappointment of such half-informed scholars, we find frequent references being made to conception Lagna and its relationship to the birth ascendant and how by taking into consideration the conception horoscope, predictions affecting the future of an individual could be attempted with sufficient accuracy. In the course of these *Studies*, I do not propose to deal with the *Nisheka Lagna* exhaustively. I would just make a casual reference to the theory as propounded by Parasara and for a fuller treatment of the subject I would refer the readers to *Brihat Parasara Hora*.

26. Parasara's Method

Jaimini does not give any particular method for finding the conception time from the birth horoscope. Therefore I shall make a reference to Parasara's method, which is as follows :—Add the distance from the Sun to Mandi, to the distance from the first to ninth house. The Sun in terms of signs, etc., counted backwards represents in terms of months the interval between the time of birth and the time of conception.

27. Samarsingh's Method

In a work entitled *Manushya Jataka*, reference is made to Adhana Lagna by the author Samarsingh who says that when the longitudes of Lagna and the Moon in the birth horoscope are the same, the period of gestation would be 273 days. When the Moon and Lagna are opposite, the duration of pregnancy would be 258 days.

28. Unsatisfactory Nature of Existing Methods

Almost all the methods of deriving Adhana Lagna from Janma Lagna, now in vogue, appear to be riddle with inconsistencies. Quite a lot of research work has to be done before a workable system could be laid down for universal acceptance. The clue is to be found in Varahamihira's reference to the correspondence between Janma Lagna and Adhana Lagna hinted at in stanza 21, Ch. IV of *Brihat Jataka*. In the absence of a fool-proof and systematic method of determining Adhana Lagna, we could safely apply the combinations suggested in Adhyaya IV by Jaimini to birth horoscopes. The principles involved in tracing the time of conception from the time of birth and *vice versa* are astronomico-biological and here is a fertile field open to scholars for investigation.

29. Pranapada

The theory of Pranapada appears to have been based on the law of periodicity according to which human, animal and vegetable births could occur only at certain definite intervals. Consequently there is a recognisable connection between the Lagna and the Pranapada sign. A good many astrologers in North India take it for granted that the Pranapada theory is the master-key for the determination of the correct time of birth. No single method can exclusively claim for itself infallibility or universal applicability. Each horoscope requires an individual approach. Parasara clearly suggests that in the matter of birth rectification Pranapada, Chandra and Gulika have all to be considered. Pranapada is a sensitive point arrived at by a certain manipulation of the birth time.

30. Method of finding Pranapada

Pranapada can be obtained by adding twice the birth-time in vighatis to (*a*) the Sun's longitude or (*b*) the Sun's longitude + 240° or (*c*) the Sun's longitude + 120° according as the Sun is in a movable, fixed or common sign, multiples of 360° being invariably expunged.

Example 8

Find the Pranapada Lagna in the Standard Horoscope.

Birth Time = Gh. 14—30 = 870 vighatis.

Sun's longitude = 301° 12′ or 1° 12′ in Aquarius, a fixed sign.

Applying the above formula, Pranapada Lagna is obtained thus :—

(2 × Birth time in vighatis) + (Sun's longitude + 240°)

= (2 × 870) + (301° 12′ + 240°)

= 1740° + 541° 12′ = 2281° 12′.

Expunging multiples of 360°, we get 121° 12′

∴ Pranapada Lagna = Simha 1° 12′.

31. Dwara Rasi

The sign in which a Dasa begins or the sign whose Dasa is under consideration is the Dwara Rasi.

Suppose the Dasa of Mesha Rasi is under consideration either for determining Maraka or some other event. Then that Rasi becomes the Dwara Rasi.

32. Bahya Rasi

The sign which is as many signs away from Dwara Rasi as the latter is from Lagna goes under the name of Bahya Rasi. Suppose Lagna is Cancer and the Rasi under consideration for purpose of maraka determination is Thula. Then Thula is Dwara Rasi. As Thula is the 4th from Lagna, the 4th from Thula, *viz.*, Makara would be the Bahya Rasi. Therefore, if Dwara is the 2nd from Lagna, Bahya would be the 3rd.

If Dwara is the	3rd,	Bahya would be	5th.
do.	4th,	do.	7th.
do.	5th,	do.	9th.
do.	6th,	do.	11th.
do.	7th,	do.	1st.
do.	8th,	do.	3rd.
do.	9th,	do.	5th.
do.	10th,	do.	7th.
do.	11th,	do.	9th.
do.	12th,	do.	11th.
do.	1st,	do.	1st.

33. Paka and Bhoga Rasis

Dwara Rasi is also known as Paka Rasi while Bahya Rasi goes under the name of Bhoga Rasi. Both these Rasis will be found to be useful mainly in the determination of longevity.

34. Gulika

The position of Gulika is important as it is frequently referred to by Jaimini especially in the matter of determination of profession. Readers must not mix up Gulika with Mandi. The position of Gulika is obtained thus: Divide the duration of day into 8 equal parts. The first seven parts are ruled by the seven planets beginning from the lord of the weekday concerned. The 8th part has no lord. The longitude of Gulika corresponds to the longitude of ascendant rising at the end of Saturn's part. Suppose the position of Gulika is required on a Friday and suppose the duration of day is 30 ghatis. Each part is equal to $3\frac{3}{4}$ ghatis. The ruler of the 1st part is Venus lord of the weekday, and that of the 2nd part (upto $7\frac{1}{2}$ ghatis) is Saturn. Therefore Gulika's longitude corresponds to the rising degree at $7\frac{1}{2}$ ghatis after sunrise.

In case of a night birth, divide the duration of night into 8 equal parts. The first seven parts are ruled by the seven planets beginning from the lord of 5th weekday from the weekday concerned. The 8th has no lord. Here again Gulika's position corresponds to the ending portion of Saturn's part of the night.

Example 9

Find the longitude of Gulika in the Standard Horoscope.

Duration of Day, *viz.*, Gh. 28.4 divided by 8 gives Gh. 3.55.

Weekday of birth is Tuesday.

∴ Saturn's part extends from Gh. 14-12 to 17-45.

Gulika's position corresponds to the rising degree at Gh. 17-45, *viz.*, Mithuna 4° 26′.

35. Brahma

In the matter of finding Sthira Dasa (art. 91 and also the period of Maraka, the planet becoming Brahma plays a very important part. Brahma is a certain distinction which a planet obtains by virtue of certain qualifications as per details given below :—

I. If the lord of the 8th from Atmakaraka is in the 8th therefrom, he becomes qualified for the position of Brahma.

II. Ascertain whether Lagna or the 7th house is stronger. Call this A.

Find the strongest of the lords of the 6th, 8th and 12th from A. Call this B.

B becomes qualified for the position of Brahma if he occupies an odd sign which should have reference to the visible* half of the zodiac.

36. Exceptions

If Saturn, Rahu or Ketu becomes eligible as per article 35 for the place of Brahma, he becomes a nominal Brahma and is automatically disqualified. The real Brahma will be the 6th planet from the nominal Brahma, counted in the order of Sun, Moon, Mars, Mercury, Jupiter, Venus, Saturn, Rahu and Ketu.

37. Selection of Brahma

When two or three planets become eligible for the position of Brahma, then select one with higher longitude. In respect of Rahu, however, the longitude must be measured from the last point of the sign. When two planets qualified to become Brahma have the same longitude, then select Brahma by Rasi Bala (see art. 52).

Example 10

Find Brahma Graha in the Standard Horoscope.

---

* From Lagna, "visible half" means the 12th to 7th houses reckoned backwards. For the 7th, "visible half" means 6th to Lagna counted backwards.

Between Lagna and 7th, Lagna is stronger = (A) (*vide* Example 18).

Lords of 6, 8 and 12 from A are Venus, Jupiter and Mars respectively.

Jupiter is the strongest because his longitude is the highest (B).

Jupiter is in an odd sign and occupies the visible horizon. Hence Jupiter is Brahma.

P.S.—No other planet becomes qualified for this position.

38. Maheswara

The lord of the 8th house from Atmakaraka is the Maheswara.

If the 8th lord from Atmakaraka is exalted or in his own house, then Maheswara would be the stronger of the lords of 8th and 12th from Atmakaraka.

When Rahu and Ketu join Atmakaraka or are in the 8th from Atmakaraka, then the 6th planet from the Sun becomes the Maheswara.

When two or more planets compete for the post of Maheswara, choose the strongest one.

Example 11

Find Maheswara in the Standard Horoscope.

The lord of the 8th from Atmakaraka is Mercury. Hence he is the Maheshwara. Neither the 8th lord is exalted nor is in his own house nor Rahu or Ketu has joined Atmakaraka or the 8th from it. Consequently there are no other competitors.

39. Rudra

The stronger of the lords of the 8th and 2nd from Lagna becomes Rudra. The other, *i.e.*, the weaker, if aspected by malefics can also become nominal or supplemental Rudra.

Example 12

Find Rudra in the Standard Horoscope.

The lord of the 8th and 2nd from Lagna are Jupiter and Mercury. Jupiter is stronger than Mercury. Hence Jupiter is Rudra.

CHAPTER III

Aspects and Argalas

40. Reckoning of Aspects

According to Hindu Astrology aspects are generally reckoned with reference to signs, even though in the determination of Drug bala or aspect-strength, the aspect angles are invariably considered. A planet cannot aspect another planet or Bhava with 30° in front of it and 60° behind it. The aspect begins from 30° in front of a planet and it stops short at the 300th degree from the planet.

41. Aspects in Jaimini

So far as Jaimini is concerned, it looks as though the aspect angles are ignored.

All movable signs aspect all fixed signs, except the adjacent ones. All fixed signs aspect all movable signs except the adjacent ones. Common signs aspect each other. To be more clear, Aries aspects the fixed signs of Leo, Scorpio and Aquarius and not Taurus, an adjacent sign. Likewise Taurus aspects Cancer, Libra and Capricorn and not Aries, an adjacent sign. The various aspects can be thus summarised to facilitate easy understanding.

Aspecting sign		*Aspected sign*
Aries aspects	...	Leo, Scorpio and Aquarius.
Taurus aspects	....	Cancer, Libra and Capricorn.
Gemini aspects	...	Virgo, Sagittarius and Pisces.

Aspecting sign		*Aspected sign*
Cancer aspects	...	Scorpio, Aquarius and Taurus.
Leo aspects	...	Libra, Capricorn and Aries.
Virgo aspects	...	Sagittarius, Pisces and Gemini.
Libra aspects	...	Aquarius, Taurus and Leo.
Scorpio aspects	...	Capricorn, Aries and Cancer.
Sagittarius aspects	...	Pisces, Gemini and Virgo.
Capricorn aspects	...	Taurus, Leo and Scorpio.
Aquarius aspects	...	Aries, Cancer and Libra.
Pisces aspects	...	Gemini, Virgo and Sagittarius.

42. Range of Aspect

In other words a Chara Rasi or a planet in it aspects the 5th, 8th and 11th from it. A Sthira Rasi or a planet in it aspects the 3rd, 6th and 9th from it, and a Dwiswabhava Rasi or a planet in it aspects the 4th, 7th and 10th from it. The range of aspects may be said to be in respect of

(*a*) Movable Signs	...	120°, 210°, 300°
(*b*) Fixed Signs	...	60°, 150°, 240°
(*c*) Common Signs	...	90°, 180°, 270°

Example 13

Tabulate the aspects in the Standard Horoscope.

The Sun is in Aquarius, a fixed sign and therefore aspects Aries (and Rahu and Moon in it), Cancer and Libra (and Kuja and Ketu in it). Similarly reckoned, the following is the table of aspects in the Standard Horoscope :

Aspecting Lord	*Aspected Lord*	*Aspected Sign*
The Sun	Rahu, Moon Mars, Ketu	Aries, Cancer Libra.
The Moon	Sun, Mercury, Jupiter	Leo Scorpio Aquarius.
Mars	Sun, Mercury, Jupiter, Lagna.	Aquarius, Taurus Leo,

Aspecting Lord	*Aspected Lord*	*Aspected Sign*
Mercury	... Same as Sun	... Same as Sun.
Jupiter	... do	... do.
Venus	... Saturn	... Pisces, Gemini and Virgo.
Saturn	... Venus	... Virgo, Sagittarius and Pisces.
Rahu	... Same as Moon	... Same as Moon.
Ketu	... Same as Moon	... Same as Mars.

43. Argalas

Planets and Rasis aspect other planets and signs according to their dispositions. These aspect influences are *affected* for good or bad by the presence, from an aspecting lord or sign, of planets in certain places. These 'affecting' or influencing agencies are called Argalas.

44. Formation of Argala

Planets in the 4th, 2nd, 11th and 5th from an aspecting body (except Ketu) cause or become Argalas. Lords who are in the 9th from Ketu become Argalas.

45. Benefic Argalas

Natural benefics in the above-mentioned place act as Benefic Argalas or augmentary agents.

46. Malefic Argalas

Natural malefics in the places mentioned in article 44 function as Malefic Argalas or obstructing agents.

Natural malefics in the 3rd can also become Argalas. The interpretation of the sutra bearing on this particular point by the commentators is neither clear nor convincing. The consensus of opinion is that Argala could be caused only when there are *many malefics* in the 3rd and not when there are one or two.

47. Counteraction of Argalas

The Argalas, generated by the disposition of planets in the 4th, 2nd, 11th and 5th from an aspecting lord or house, get neutralised or counteracted by the simultaneous presence of planets in the 10th, 12th, 3rd or 9th respec tively from the aspecting body concerned. With reference to Ketu a planet in the 5th removes the Argala given rise to by the presence of a planet in the 9th.

Elucidating the same point further, we can say that an Argala caused by the situation of a planet in the 4th gets cancelled by the presence of a planet in the 10th; the Argala produced by a planet's disposition in the 2nd is emoved by the presence of a planet in the 12th and that- of the 11th is cancelled by the 3rd and that of the 5th by the 9th. In other words, the Argala points, 4, 2, 11 and 5 have as their counteracting points 10, 12, 3 and 9 respectively. It will be seen that the Argala, caused by the presence of *malefics* in the 3rd, has no neutralising agency. It is a purely Malefic Argala, which could be given rise to only when there are a number of malefics. The following schedule will further clear the Argala question :

Argala Place	*Counteracting Places*	*Nature of Argala*
4	10	Benefic or Malefic
2	12	
11	3	
3	...	Malefic
5	9	Benefic or Malefic
9 (Ketu)	5	

If a planet obstructing Argala is weaker than a planet causing Argala, or is less in longitude, the Argala cannot be counteracted.

48. Significance of Argalas

Fortunate results will be conferred in the Dasas *(see* article 128) of Rasis in which Benefic Argalas are caused. Evil results will befall during Dasas of Rasis in which Papargalas have been centered. If the Benefic Argalas have reference to, *i.e.*, fall in Pada Lagna, Lagna or the 7th and are not neutralised, the person becomes highly fortunate and wealthy.

49. Argala Chakra

This can be cast by taking into consideration the Argala caused with reference to each Rasi by the presence of planets in places mentioned in article 44. Thus if in a horoscope, from Aries, a planet is in the 4th, causing Argala we can put the planet in Aries in the Argala Chakra.

Example 14

Find the Argalas and their neutralisation in the Standard Horoscope.

Taking the Sun in the Standard Horoscope, we find that the 4th and 2nd are vacant. The 3rd is not occupied by a large number of malefics. The fifth is occupied by Venus, causing Subhargala. The Malefic Argala caused by Saturn in the 5th from the Sun is neutralised by the presence of Mars in the 9th. The Benefic Argala caused by Venus in the 11th is neutralised by the presence of the Moon and Ketu in the 3rd. As, however, the Argala causing Saturn (3° 20′) and Venus (20° 33′) have greater longitude than their respective Argala-destroying agents

Chandra (Ravi, Budha, *Guru*) Rahu (Ravi, Budha, *Guru*) Sani (*Sukra*)	Ravi (*Sani*) Budha (Sani) Guru (Sani)	Sani (*Chandra, Rahu*)	Kuja (*Ravi, Budha, Guru*) Ketu (Ravi, Budha, Guru) Chandra Rahu
Sani (Kuja, *Ketu*) Sukra (Chandra, *Rahu*)	ARGALA CHAKRA		Kuja (*Chandra, Rahu*) Ketu (Chandra, *Rahu*)
Ravi (*Sukra*) Budha (*Sukra*) Guru (Sukra) Chandra (Kuja, *Ketu*) Rahu (Kuja, *Ketu*)			Sukra (Chandra, *Rahu*) Sani (Kuja, *Ketu*)
Chandra Rahu Kuja (*Ravi, Budha, Guru*) Ketu (Ravi, Budha Guru)	Sukra (Kuja, *Ketu*) Ravi Budha Guru	Ravi (*Sani*) Budha (Sani) Guru (Sani)	Kuja Ketu Sukra (Sani)

Mars (0° 53′) and Moon (18° 29′) we can assume that there is no neutralisation of Argala.

50. Argala Chart in the Standard Horoscope

Planets not enclosed in brackets have caused Argalas. Those enclosed in brackets are the counteracting ones. Planets in *italics* are those that have actually asserted their counteracting influences. Take Mesha in the above chart. Ravi, Budha and Guru have caused Argalas which though counteracted by Sani have not been completely neutralised. Take Vrishabha. Argala is caused by Sani, but it is counteracted by the Moon. The Moon being stronger than Sani (because of having lesser longitude), there is complete neutralisation of the Argala. Take Mithuna. Argala has been generated by (*a*) Rahu and Chandra and (*b*) Kuja and Ketu. That caused by Rahu and Chandra has not been obstructed. But the Argala caused by Kuja and Ketu (because of their positions in the 5th from Mithuna) has been cancelled by Ravi, Budha and Guru (because of their position in the 9th from Mithuna). But actually, the Argala influence is not cancelled *in toto* because of the Argala producing bodies, *e.g.*, Ketu is stronger than Guru while the Argala destroying Budha is stronger than Kuja.

Planetary Argalas in the Standard Horoscope.

Planet		*Argala caused by*		*Argala counteracted by*
The Sun	....	Sani, Sukra	....	Kuja, Ketu. Chandra, Rahu.
The Moon	....	Ravi, *Budha, Guru*	...	Sani
Mars	....	Ravi, *Budha, Guru*	...	Sani

Planet		*Argala caused by*		*Argala counteracted by*
Mercury	...	Same as Sun	...	Same as Sun
Jupiter	...	Do	...	Do
Venus	...	*Chandra, Rahu,* Kuja *Ketu*	...	Ravi, Budha, Guru
Saturn	...	Do	...	Do
Rahu	...	Same as Moon	...	Same as Moon
Ketu	...	Sani	...	Ravi, Budha, Guru

Planets *in italics* have caused Argalas but there is no neutralisation either because of the weakness of the counteracting planet or the obsence of the counteracting planet in the appropriate place. Take for instance Mars. Argala is eaused by Ravi, Budha and Guru in the 5th. Though a planet is situated in the 9th, he cannot neutralise the Argala completely because of the fact of his being weak and isolated.

Note for instance the Argala caused to the 7th house by the situation of the Sun, Mercury and Jupiter. The native was wealthy, fortunate and influential.

CHAPTER IV

Planetary and Rasi Strengths

51. Sources of Strength

In Parasari, the strength of a planet is numerically measurable, and consists of six kinds or varieties. These have been explained at considerable length in my book *Graha and Bhava Balas* and I do not therefore propose to say anything about this subject in the course of this book. Determination of Shadbalas involves elaborate calculations. Jaimini on the other hand dispenses with all cumbersome calculations and the methods formulated for ascertaining planetary and house strengths are simple. In the determination of longevity, planetary and house strengths play an important role. It must be noted that Jaimini lays greater emphasis on the strengths of Rasis, which is always derived by the position of one or more planets in it. As Jaimini does not recognise the distinction between Rasi and Bhava, the meaning of these two words in the context of Jaimini's principles may be considered to be synonymous.

52. Sources of Rasi Strength

The clue for determining strengths of planets and Rasis is to be found in Adhyaya 2, Pada 3 of *Jaimini Sutras*. A careful study of the relevant sutras reveals that the subject of Rasi strengths can be classified into six distinct categories, *viz*., (*a*) Strength due to Atmakaraka, (*b*) Association strength, (*c*) Location or Aspect strength, (*d*) Strength due to the lord, (*e*) Strength of odd signs and (*f*) Atmakaraka-disposition strength. We shall explain each one of these clearly. For an improvised method of my own, I would refer the readers to article 62.

53. Atmakaraka Strength

Since Atmakaraka is the most important planet in a horoscope, the Rasi holding him becomes the strongest.

54. Association Strength

This is based upon the presence or absence of planets in a Rasi and the Rasi strength is measured thus:

(*a*) A Rasi occupied by a planet is stronger than a Rasi that have no planet in it.

(*b*) In case to Rasis have planets in them, that which has a larger number is stronger than the one having a lesser number.

(*c*) If Rasis have an equal number of planets posited in them, then measure their respective strengths by considering whether the planets are exalted, or are in Moolathrikona; in own or friendly or neutral or inimical houses, the planet in exaltation being the strongest, that in Moolathrikona being less strong, that in own house being strong, that in a friendly sign less strong, that in a neutral sign still less strong and that in debility or inimical house being the least powerful. Thus, if two Rasis have two planets in each, and one planet is *neecha* in one Rasi and the other planet is *uchha* in the other Rasi, then the Rasi with the *uchha* planet becomes the stronger.

(*d*) If strength of two Rasis is equal as determined according to (*a*), (*b*) and (*c*), then the strength must be ascertained by taking into consideration the Chara, Sthira or Dwiswabhave nature of the Rasi. A Sthira Rasi is stronger than a Chara Rasi and Dwiswabhava Rasi is stronger than a Sthira Rasi.

55. Location or Aspect Strength

The Rasi could become strong by the conjunction or aspect of Jupiter, Mercury or its won lord.

56. Strength due to Lord

Out of two Rasis, that whose lord has greater strength as per articles 59 and 60 becomes stronger.

57. Strength of Odd Rasis

When it is a question of measuring the strengths of two Rasis both of which are odd, that which has planets on either side should be considered the stronger of the two.

58. Atmakaraka Disposition Strength

Rasis, whose lords occupy Kendra, Panapara and Apoklima from Atmakaraka, get full strength, half strength and feeble strength respectively.

59. Sources of Planetary Strength

There are two sources of planetary strength, *viz.*, (*a*) Amsa bala and (*b*) Moolathrikona bala.

60. Amsa Bala

Amsa means longitude and bala means strength. A planet whose longitude (from the beginning of the sign) is greater than that of another planet, becomes stronger than the latter. Suppose the longitude of the Sun is 25° Aries and that of Mars 18° Cancer. The Sun is stronger than Mars.

61. Moolathrikona Bala

This has reference to the situation of a planet in an inimical (satrukshetra), debilitated (neecha), neutral (sama), friendly (mithrakshetra), own (swakshetra), moolathrikona or exaltation (uchha) Rasis.

A planet in exaltation becomes the strongest and that in debilitation the weakest, the strength decreasing from exaltation to debilitation in the descending order thus :

Exaltation, Moolathrikona, own sign, friendly sign, neutral sign, inimical sign and debilitation sign.

In applying the rules for the determination of planetary strengths, the order mentioned above should be observed. As in ordinary Astrology, one has to make a careful study of the principles, understand them thoroughly and then apply them to a number of horoscopes so that one could get sufficient practical experience.

Example 15

Determine the Rasi Srengths in the Standard Horoscope.

I. Aries and Libra :—

(*a*) Both have two planets each and both are Chara.

(*b*) Both are aspected by Jupiter and Mercury.

(*c*) The Moon in Mesha is in a neutral sign while Kuja in Thula is also in a neutral sign.

(*d*) Kuja lord of Mesha and Sukra lord of Thula occupy respectively Apoklima and Panapara Rasis from Atmakaraka. Thula is stronger than Mesha.

(*e*) Venus lord of Libra is stronger than Mars lord of Mesha. Hence Libra is stronger than Mesha.

II Gemini and Sagittarius :—

(*a*) Both have a planet each and both are Dwiswabhava.

(*b*) Gemini aspected by Venus, a friend. Dhanus aspected by Saturn, a neutral.

(*c*) Saturn in Mithuna is in a friend's sign, Venus is in the house of a neutral.

(*d*) Budha lord of Mithuna is in a Kendra from Atmakaraka but Guru is Atmakaraka himself.

(*e*) The lord of Dhanus is stronger than the lord of Mithuna.

Hence Dhanus is stronger than Mithuna.

III. Aquarius :—Has the largest number of planets besides being occupied by Atmakaraka. Both Sun and Mercury are also posited here. Consequently it is the strongest Rasi.

62. Numerical Measure of Rasi Strength

Above I have given as clearly as possible the sources of strength of Rasis. It occurs to me that unless some method, akin to the one suggested by Parasara, is devised, it would be rather difficult to categorically say, which is the strongest or which is the weakest Rasi. The whole technique of Dasa prediction according to Jaimini hinges on the Rasis and their relative strengths. Based upon the principles adumbrated in articles 52 to 61 and making a slight departure from Jaimini, or to be more correct, adapting the relevant principles from Parasari, I have devised the following improvised method of numerically determining the strengths of the various Rasis. Readers must clearly bear in mind that the method is offered as a possible solution of the problem of evaluating strengths and it may be rejected by those who may find the method arbitrary or who may not favour the idea of the slightest departure from Jaimini. It is given for what it is worth.

From the details furnished in articles 52 to 61 it is clear that the strength of a Rasi is made up of (i) the lord's strength and (ii) the Rasi's own strength derived from (*a*) the cardinal, fixed or common nature of the sign which I would call Chara bala, (*b*) the sign having the aspect or association of Jupiter, Mercury or its own lord —Druk bala and (*c*) the fact of the sign being occupied by one or more planets—Sthira Bala. We can therefore say that the total strength of Rasi is the (*a*) sum of its own strength *plus* (*b*) that of the lord. We shall take up these two items separately.

63. The Lord's Strength

So far as the lord's strength is concerned, it may be assumed to be made up of strength due to (i) his residence in exaltation sign, own house, etc., which I would call Moolathrikona bala, (ii) the longitudinal position—Amsa bala and (iii) situation in Kendra, Panapara and Apoklima from Atmakaraka—Kendra bala.

64. Moolathrikona Bala

Let not the reader mix this up with Moolathrikona bala discussed in my *Graha and Bhava Balas* where a consideration of a planet's situation in a friendly, inimical, own place, etc., in all the Saptha Vargas is required.

Here the reference is only to Rasi Chart. The lord of a sign (whose strength is to be found) may occupy an exaltation place, Moolathrikona, own house, etc. We can assign for these different situations the following numerical values in terms of shashtiamsas :—

Exaltation	...	...	60.00
Moolathrikona	...	...	45.00

Own House	...	...	30.00
Friend's House	...	...	22.50
Neutral's House	...	...	15.00
Enemy's House	....	...	7.40
Debilitation	...	...	3.75

65. Amsa Bala

By Amsa is meant the degree of longitude held by a planet. According to article 60 a planet with a higher longitude is stronger than a planet with a lower longitude. Extending the same principle further, we can say that the planet holding the highest longitude would be the strongest and the one with the lowest the weakest, the strength decreasing in the descending order of the longitudes. Excluding the nodes, we have seven planets whose lordship alone over the 12 signs is considered for purposes of strength-determination. As the planet with the highest longitude would be the strongest we could arbitrarily assign 60 shashtiamsas as its Amsa bala while for the weakest 3.75 units may be assigned, the other planets being given the following values :—

(1)	The planet that has advanced most in a sign	...	60.00	shashtiamsas.
(2)	Less advanced than (1)	...	45.00	"
(3)	Less than (2)	...	30.00	"
(4)	Less than (3)	....	22.50	"
(5)	Less than (4)	....	15.00	"
(6)	Less than (5)	...	7.50	"
(7)	The least advanced	...	3.75	"

66 Kendra Bala

Article 58 says that the Rasi, whose lord is in a Kendra, Panapara, or Apoklima, from Atmakaraka, gets full strength, ordinary strength and feeble strength. Therefore, we can assign the following values as Kendra bala :—

A planet in a Kendra from Atmakaraka—60 shashtiamsas.

A planet in a Panapara from Atmakaraka—30 shashtiamsas.

A planet in an Apoklima from Atmakaraka—15 shashtiamsas.

Example 16

Find Moolathrikona bala, Amsa bala and Kendra bala of the various planets in the Standard Horoscope.

The Sun.—(*a*) He is in Kumbha, an enemy's house. His Moolathrikona bala is 7.5 units.

(*b*) According to longitudinal position, the Sun is the 6th (see Ex. 1). Hence his Amsa bala is 7.50 units.

(*c*) The Sun is in a Kendra (1st) from Atmakaraka. His Kendra bala is 60.0 units.

∴ The total strength of the Sun is :

Moolathrikona	...	7.5
Amsa	...	7.5
Kendra	...	60.0
Total	...	75.0 shashtiamsas.

Dealing with the other planets similarly, we can enter their strengths in a tabular form thus :—

Planet	*Moolathrikona Bala*	*Amsa Bala*	*Kendra Bala*	*Total*
The Sun	... 7.50 (Satru)	7.50	60.00	75.00
The Moon	... 15.00 (Neutral)	30.00	15.00	60.00
Mars	... 15.00 (Neutral)	3.75	15.00	33.75

Planet	*Moolathrikona Bala*	*Amsa Bala*	*Kendra Bala*	*Total*
Mercury	... 15.00 (Neutral)	22.50	60.00	97.50
Jupiter	... 15.00 (Neutral)	60.00	60.00	135.00
Venus	... 15.00 (Neutral)	45.00	30.00	90.00
Saturn	.... 22.00 (Mitra)	15.00	30.00	67.50

67. Chara Bala

From article 54 (*d*) it is clear that a Dwiswabhava Rasi is more powerful than a Sthira Rasi and that a Sthira Rasi is more powerful than a Chara Rasi. We can therefore assign the following values of strength :—

Dwiswabhava Rasi	...	60	shashtiamsas.
Sthira Rasi	...	30	"
Chara Rasi	...	15	"

68. Druk Bala

This has reference to article 55. A Rasi aspected by (or associated with) its own lord, or Jupiter or Mercury is rendered strong. We can therefore say that when a Rasi is aspected by or associated with

Jupiter, it gets a Druk bala of 60 units.
Mercury, it gets a Druk bala of 60 units.
Its own lord, it gets a Druk bala of 60 units.

69. Sthira Bala

A Rasi with two planets is stronger than the one with one planet. That with three is stronger than that with two and so on. There are seven lords and 2 nodes. Very rarely do more than 7 planets and Rahu or Ketu can stay in a single sign. We can therefore arbitarily assign the following numerical values :—

When 8 planets are in a sign	...	165 shashtiamsas.
do. 7 do.	...	150 "
do. 6 do.	...	135 "
do. 5 do.	...	120 "
do. 4 do.	...	105 "
do. 3 do.	...	90 "
do. 2 do.	...	75 "
do. 1 planet is in a sign	...	60 "
When no planet		0 "

Take Mesha :—

(*a*) *Chara Bala* :—It is a Chara Rasi. Its Chara bala is 15 shashtiamsas.

(*b*) *Druk bala* :—It is aspected both by Guru and Budha and gets a total of 120 shashtiamsas as Druk bala.

(*c*) *Sthira Bala* :—Two planets, *viz.*, Chandra and Rahu occupy Mesha. Therefore, Sthira bala is 75 shashtiamsas.

Mesha's own strength is : 15 + 120 + 75 = 210 shashtiamsas.

The following is the schedule of Rasis' own strength in the Standard Horoscope:—

Rasi	Chara bala	Druk bala	Sthira bala	Rasi's own strength
Mesha	— 15.00	60.00 60.00	75.00	210.00
Vrishabha	— 30.00	—	—	30.00
Mithuna	— 60.00	—	60.00	120.00
Kataka	— 15.00	60.00 60.00	—	135.00
Simha	— 30.00	—	—	30.00

Rasi	Chara bala	Druk bala	Sthira bala	Rasi's own strength
Kanya	— 60.00	—	—	60.00
Thula	— 15.00	60.00 60.00	75.00	210.00
Vrischika	— 30.00	—	—	30.00
Dhanus	— 60.00	—	60.00	120.00
Makara	— 15.00	—	—	15.00
Kumbha	— 30.00	60.00 60.00	90.00	240.00
Meena	— 60.00	—	—	60.00

70. Total Rasi Strength

The total strength of Rasi is the sum-total of Rasi's own strength and that of the lord. Thus in the Standard Horoscope, the total strength of Mesha is :

Strength of lord	...	33.75	shashtiamsas
Rasi's own strength	...	210.00	,,
Total	...	243.75	,,

71. Special Strength

In addition to the above, a Rasi can get 60 shashtiamsas of special strength if it happens to house the Atmakaraka. This is generally got by only one Rasi.

Example 18

Find the total strength of Rasis in the Standard Horoscope.

Rasi		Strength of lord	Rasi's own strength	Total strength of the Rasi
Mesha	...	33.75	210.00	243.75
Vrishabha	...	90.00	30.00	120.00
Mithuna	...	97.50	120.00	217.50
Kataka	...	60.00	135.00	195.00
Simha	...	75.00	30.00	105.00
Kanya	...	97.50	60.00	157.50
Thula	...	90.00	210.00	300.00
Vrischika	...	33.75	30.75	63.75
Dhanus	...	135.00	120.00	255.00
Makara	...	67.50	15.00	82.50
Kumbha	...	67.50	240.00 *60.00	367.50
Meena	....	135.00	60.00	195.00

In the Standard Horoscope, the following are the strengths of Rasis in their descending order :—

Kumbha	...	367.50	Strongest	I
Thula	...	300.00		II
Dhanus	...	255.00		III
Mesha	...	243.75		IV
Mithuna	...	217.50		V
Meena	...	195.00 }		IV
Kataka	...	195.00 }		
Kanya	...	157.50		VII
Vrishabha	...	120.00		VIII
Simha	...	105.00		IX
Makara	...	82.50 }	Weakest	X
Vrischika	...	63.75 }		

* Add 60 shashtiamsas for Kumbha as Atmakaraka Guru is in it.

72. Exceptions

Where the Sage has specifically mentioned that the strength of a Rasi for purposes of certain specific predictions, should be determined according to the longitudes covered by the lords, etc., the method suggested above should not be applied at all.

CHAPTER V

Dasas and Bhuktis

73. Kinds of Dasas

Just as in Parasari, there are a number of Dasas mentioned in Jaimini. Whilst Parasara's scheme of Dasas is almost entirely based upon the planets and their dispositions in certain constellations, Jaimini's Dasas invariably refer to Rasis. In calculating the Dasas of Jaimini one is likely to get confused, owing to the methods of counting one has to employed to arrive at Dasas and Bhukti periods. A little oversight may upset the whole scheme of a particular Dasa and lead the student into erroneous deductions. One must therefore be careful in checking and rechecking the Dasa calulations before attempting predictions.

Jaimini makes mention of the following Dasas :—

(1) *Chara Dasa*, (2) *Sthira Dasa*, (3) *Thrikona Dasa*, (4) *Sula Dasa*, (5) *Ravi Dasa*, (6) *Kendra Dasa*, (7) *Varnada Dasa*, (8) *Udu Dasa*, (9) *Navamsa Dasa*, (10) *Brahma Dasa*, (11) *Yogardha Dasa*, (12) *Drig Dasa*, (13) *Nakshatra Dasa and* (14) *Mandooka Dasa*.

74. Choice of Dasa

No definite clue is given by the Sage as to the specific conditions under which the different Dasas should be applied for purposes of prediction. Casual references made here and there, that an event such as for instance mother's death would happen in a certain Thrikona Dasa, should guide us in the selection of the appropriate Dasas for appropriate events. As most readers would perhaps be aware, whilst Parasara mentions a variety of Dasas, the pride of place is invariably given to Vimshottari and experience warrants this. My grandfather late Prof. B. Suryanarain Rao used to tell me that Chara Dasa and Thrikona Dasa could be applied to all horoscopes and that all important human events could be timed with sufficient accuracy with the aid of Navamsa Dasa, while for longevity purposes, his choice was Chara Dasa or Niryana Shula Dasa. Since Astrology is a practical science, dogmatic assertions, as to the suitability of this or that system of Dasa, just because it is a favourite of an eminent scholar are uncalled for. The choice must be left to the discretion of the intelligent reader who should be guided not only by his own experience but by that of scholars who have made a life-long study of the subject. I am personally inclined to favour both Chara and Sthira Dasas. This conclusion is, of course, based upon my own meagre studies.

I do not therefore propose to detail all the Dasas mentioned above in the course of this book. I shall deal with Chara Dasa exhaustively and make brief references to Thrikona Dasa, Sthira Dasa, Rasi Dasa, Brahma Dasa, Varnada Dasa and Niryana Shula Dasas.

75. Chara Dasa

This particular system appears to be a favourite with the Sage. Rasis have been divided in to two groups, *viz.*, Vishamapada (odd group) and Samapada (even group) for purposes of reckoning the order of succession of Dasa and counting the Dasa years.

76. Vishamapada Rasis

Aries, Tausus, Gemini, Libra, Scorpio and Sagittarius belong to the odd group (Vishamapada).

77. Samapada Rasis

Cancer, Leo, Virgo, Capricorn, Aquarius and Pisces belong to the even group (Samapada). For purposes of clarity, we shall use the terms Savya group and Apasavya group to denote the signs mentioned in articles 76 and 77 respectively.

78. The Order of Dasas

When the 9th house from Lagna refers to a sign in the Savya group, the order of Dasa succession would be direct or clockwise, the first Dasa starting from Lagna Rasi. When the 9th from Lagna refers to a sign in the Apasavya group, the order of Dasa in succession would be the reverse or anti-clockwise direction, the first Dasa being that of Lagna Rasi. Suppose for example two cases where (*a*) Mesha and (*b*) Kataka are Lagnas. In the first case, the 9th house from Lagna, *viz.*, Sagittarius refers to Savya group. The first and succeeding Dasas would be in the order of Mesha, Vrishabha, etc. In the second case, the 9th house from Lagna (Karkataka) is Pisces, belonging to Apasavya group. The first and succeeding Dasas would be in the order of Kataka, Mithuna, Vrishabha, etc.

79. Dasa Period

The period of a Chara Dasa is not constant. It is variable according to the situation of a lord with reference to his Rasi. The Dasa period of a Rasi is equal to $n-1$ where n represents the distance (in terms of Rasis) between the Rasi in question and the lord thereof, counted clockwise or anti-clockwise, according as the concerned Rasi belongs to the Savya or Apasavya group. Let us take a chart where Lagna is Mesha, lord of Lagna Kuja is in Simha, Sukra is in Vrischika and Chandra is in Simha. The 9th from Lagna, *viz.*, Sagittarius, refers to Savya group. Consequently, the succession of Dasas, the first always starting from Lagna, would be in the direct order. Since Lagna is Mesha, the first Dasa in this case would be that of the Lagna Rasi. *viz.*, Mesha. The lord of Mesha, *viz.*, Kuja is in Simha. Since Mesha also belongs to Savya group, counting in the direct order from Mesha to Simha, we get *n* equal to 5. Therefore the duration of Mesha Rasi Dasa is equal to 4 years (*n—1*). Taking Vrishabha, the next Rasi Dasa : It falls under Savya group. Its lord Venus is in Vrischika. Therefore the distance (*n*) from Vrishabha to Vrischika counted in the direct order is 7 and the Dasa period of Vrishabha is (*n —1*) 6 years. The next Dasa (Mithuna) can also be similarly calculated. Now to ascertain the duration of Karkataka Dasa. Cancer falls in the Apasavya group. The lord Moon is in Simha. The counting from Cancer must be in the reverse direction, which in this case would be 12 (*n*) and the period of Cancer Dasa would be II years (*n—1*).

Let us now take a chart where Lagna is Makara, Sani, Guru and Kuja occupying Simha, Mesha and Kanya respectively. The 9th from Lagna, *viz.*, Kanya belongs to the Apasavya group. Consequently the first Dasa starting from Lagna (Makara Dasa) is succeeded by subsequent Dasas in the reverse order, *viz.*, Dhanus, Vrischika, Thula, etc. To find the duration of Makara Dasa. Its lord Sani is in Simha. As Makara is an Apasavya group sign, we get 6 (*n*) by counting from Makara to the place of Saturn in the reverse order. The duration of Makara Dasa is 5 years (*n—1*). The next Dasa Rasi Sagittarius belongs to

Savya group and the lord Jupiter is in Mesha. Therefore counting directly from Dhanus to Mesha, we get n equal to 5. The duration of Dhanus Dasa would be 4 $(n-1)$. In a similar manner Dasa periods for other Rasis should be ascertained.

80. Further Variations of Dasa Duration

Ordinarily the Dasa period is denoted by the formula given in the article 79. But the period is increased or decreased according to certain benefic and melefic dispositions of the lords. Thus if a Rasi is occupied by its own lord, then the Dasa period would be 12 years. If the Rasi lord is exalted, the Rasi Dasa period obtained as per article 79 sbould be increased by one year. If the Rasi lord is debilitated, the Rasi Dasa period is diminished by one year.

81. Variations due to Dual Lordship

It will be seen that in the scheme of Jaimini, Kumbha and Vrischika are ruled by two planets each. Kuja and Ketu own Vrischika and Sani and Rahu own Kumbha. In determining the Dasa period of Kumbha and Vrischika in view of their double lordship, certain special considerations are necessary.

82. Conjunction of Dual Lords in Own Rasi

If Kuja and Ketu, or Sani and Rahu, are in conjunction in their own houses, then the Dasa period of Vrischika and Kumbha will be 12 years each.

83. Mars-Ketu Conjunction in Other Signs

If Mars and Ketu are in conjunction in a sign other than their own, then count clockwise (as Vrischika belongs to Savya group) from Vrischika to the Rasi in question. The Dasa period of Vrischika will be as per article 79.

84. Saturn-Rahu Conjunction in Other Signs

If there is a conjunction of Rahu and Saturn in a sign other than Kumbha, then count anti-clockwise (because Kumbha refers to Apasavya group) from Kumbha to the Rasi in question. The Dasa period of Kumbha will be as per article 79.

85. One Lord in Own Rasi and the Other Lord in a Different Rasi

When one of the double-lords (Kuja or Ketu, or Sani or Rahu) is in his own sign and the other is in a different sign, ignore the former and prefer the latter. That is if Mars is in Vrischika and Ketu is in Meena, ignore Mars and prefer Ketu. The Dasa period of Vrischika will be decided by Ketu as per article 79.

86. Dual Lords in Different Rasis

When Mars and Ketu (or Saturn and Rahu) are in different Rasis, prefer the one with an associate. If both the lords are associated with other planets, prefer the one with the greater number of associates. When both the lords have an equal number of associates, prefer the one with Rasibala by taking into consideration the Chara, Sthira and Dwiswabhava nature of the Rasi (*rasitaha pranaha*). Sthira being stronger than Chara and Dwiswabhava being stronger than Sthira. If the two lords appear equal in strength, even according to Rasibala, then prefer the lord who gives the larger number of years. If per chance the lord who gives the larger number of years is over-debilitated and the other lord is exalted, prefer the latter, increasing the period by one year as per article 80.

Example 19

Final the order of the Chara Dasas and their perio' in the Standard Horoscope.

Order of Dasas :—The 9th from Lagna is Makara. It belongs to Apasavya group. Therefore, the first Dasa starting from Lagna, *viz.*, Vrishabha is continued in the reverse order, *viz.*, Vrishabha, Mesha, Meena, Kumbha, Makara, etc.

Dasa Periods :—Let us take the first Rasi Dasa, *viz.*, Taurus. It falls in the Savya group (Article 76). Therefore the counting must be in the direct order. The lord of Vrishabha, *viz.*, Sukra is in Sagittarius the 8th (*n*) from Vrishabha. Therefore the Dasa period of Vrishabha is $n-1$ or 7 years. Take Mesha, the next Dasa Rasi. It falls in the Savya group. The counting must be in the direct order. The lord of Mesha, *viz.*, Kuja is in Libra, the 7th (*n*) from Mesha. Hence the duration of Mesha Dasa is $7-1=6$ years. The third Dasa is that of Meena. It belongs to Apasavya group. The counting must therefore be in reverse order. Jupiter, lord of Meena, is in the 2nd (*n*) from Meena (counted backwards). Therefore Meena Dasa period is $2-1=1$ year. Let us take Kumbha, a sign of dual lordship. Between Rahu and Sani, both owning Kumbha, Rahu is with Chandra. Hence prefer Rahu (article 86). Kumbha falls in Apasavya group. Therefore counting from Kumbha to the sign occupied get *n* as 11. Therefore the duration of Kumbha Dasa is $11-1=10$ years. Taking Vrischika, another sign of dual lordship, we find that both Kuja and Ketu are in conjunction. Therefore as per article 83, we have to simply count (in the direct order as Vrischika refers to Savya group) from Vrischika to Thula where Kuja and Ketu are in conjunction. This gives *n* as 12, and the Dasa period of Vrischika is

12—1 = 11 years. Calculating similarly for other Rasis, the following are the Chara Dasas in the case of the Standard Horoscope :—

Dasa		*Years*
Vrishabha	...	7 0 0
Mesha	...	6 0 0
Meena	..	1 0 0
Kumbha	...	10 0 0
Makara	...	7 0 0
Dhanus	...	2 0 0
Vrischika	...	11 0 0
Thula	...	2 0 0
Kanya	...	7 0 0
Simha	...	6 0 0
Kataka	...	3 0 0
Mithuna	...	8 0 0

No Rasi is occupied by its own, exalted or debilitated lord. Therefore there is no increase or decrease of any Dasa period given above.

Example 20

Find Chara Dasas in the case of a person born on 8th August 1912 A.D. at 7-35 p.m. (I.S.T.) at Bangalore, the positions of planets at birth being as given in the chart

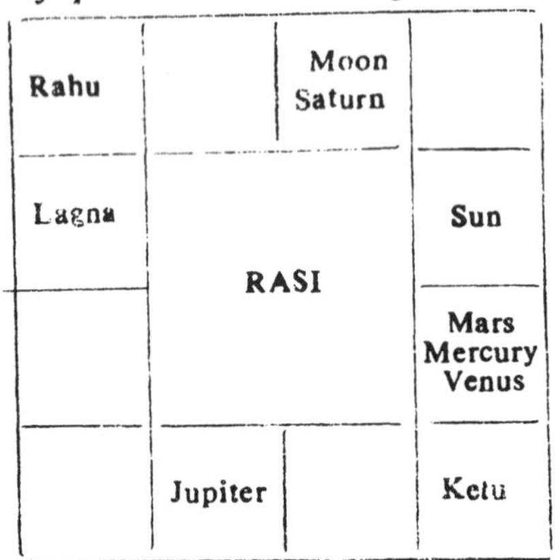

Dasa Order :—In the above horoscope, the 9th from Lagna is Thula, a sign belonging to Savya group. Consequently, the first Dasa, starting from Lagna, *viz.*, Kumbha, is continued in the direct order, *viz.*, Kumbha, Meena, Mesha, etc.

Dasa Periods :—Taking the first Dasa Rasi, *viz.*, Kumbha, we find that it is a sign of dual lordship. Saturn and Rahu are neither in conjunction nor in their own sign. They occupy different signs. Therefore applying article 86, we have to prefer Saturn, as he is associated with a planet. Kumbha falls in Apasavya group. Therefore counting (in the reverse order) from Kumbha to Saturn we get *n* as 10. Therefore the period of Kumbha is 10 − 1 = 9 years. Taking Meena, the next Dasa Rasi : It also belongs to Apasavya group. Its lord Jupiter is in Scorpio. Counting from Meena (in the reverse direction) to the place of Jupiter we get 5 as *n*. Therefore the Dasa period of Meena is 5—1 = 4. Let us take Cancer. Its lord Moon is in Taurus. Counting from Cancer to Moon (in the reverse order as Cancer belongs to Apasavya group) we get *n* as 3. Therefore (*n*—1) = 2. As lord of Cancer is exalted, the period of 2 years is to be increased by one more year (*vide* article 80). Therefore the Dasa period of Cancer is 3 years. Taking again Vrischika, a sign ruled by two lords, *viz.*, Mars and Ketu, who, in this horoscope, occupy different signs, preference should be given to Mars as he is associated with other planets while Ketu has no association. Counting from Vrischika to Kuja (in the direct order as Vrischika belongs to Savya group) we get 10 (*n*). The Dasa period of Vrischika is therefore 10—1 = 9. Similarly calculated, the following is the table of Rasi Dasas in respect of the horoscope under consideration :—

Dasa		*Years*
Kumbha	...	9 0 0
Meena	...	4 0 0
Mesha	...	4 0 0
Vrishabha	...	3 0 0
Mithuna	...	2 0 0
Kataka	...	3 0 0
Simha	...	1 0 0
Kanya	...	1 0 0
Thula	...	10 0 0
Vrischika	...	9 0 0
Dhanus	...	11 0 0
Makara	...	8 0 0

87. Bhukthis in Chara Dasa

Determination of the order of succession of the sub-periods in a Rasi Dasa is based on the same principle that is employed in deciding the order of succession of main Dasa from the first Dasa. If the 9th from the Rasi, for which the sub-periods are desired, belongs to the Savya group, then the sub-periods in that Rasi run in the direct order, the first sub-period being that of the 2nd Rasi from the Dasa Rasi. If the 9th falls in an Apasavya group, then the Bhukthis succeed in the reverse direction, the first Bhukthi being that of the 2nd Rasi (in the reverse direction) from the Dasa Rasi concerned. Suppose sub-periods in Vrishabha Rasi-Dasa are required. The 9th from Vrishabha, *viz.*, Makara belongs to the Apasavya group. Consequently, the first sub-period will be that of the 2nd Rasi (considered in the reverse order) from Taurus, *viz.*, Aries, the 2nd, 3rd and other sub-periods being Meena, Kumbha, etc., the last sub-period being that of Vrishabha itself. Suppose sub-periods from Mesha Rasi Dasa are required. The 9th from Mesha refers to Savya group. Hence the order of succession is direct. The first sub-period would be that of the 2nd Rasi (direct count) from Mesha, *viz.*, Vrishabha, the last sub-period being that of Mesha.

88. Duration of Sub-periods

As the number of periods is 12, the duration of a sub-period would be one-twelfth of the duration of a Dasa period. Thus in the Standard Horoscope, the Dasa period of Vrishabha being 7 years, each sub-period or Bhukthi extends for 7 months.

Example 21

Find out the order of Bhukthis in the Chara Dasa of Vrishabha and Mesha in the Standard Horoscopes.

As the 9th from Vrishabha refers to the Apasavya group, the succession of Bhukthis is in the converse order, the first Bhukthi being that of the 2nd from Vrishabha viz., Mesha) counted anti-clockwise. The following are the sub-periods in Vrishabha Rasi :—

Dasa		*Bhukthi*		*y. m. d.*
Vrishabha	...	Mesha	...	0 7 0
do.	...	Meena	...	0 7 0
do.	...	Kumbha	...	0 7 0
do.	..	Makara	...	0 7 0
do.	...	Dhanus	...	0 7 0
do.	...	Vrischika	...	0 7 0
do.	...	Thula	...	0 7 0
do.	...	Kanya	...	0 7 0
do.	...	Simha	...	0 7 0
do.	...	Kataka	...	0 7 0
do.	...	Mithuna	...	0 7 0
do.	...	Vrishabha	...	0 7 0
				7 0 0

Taking the next Dasa Mesha: the 9th from Mesha refers to Savya group. Therefore the succession of Bhukthis will be in the direct order. The first Bhukthi would be that of Vrishabha, the 2nd from Mesha. The duration of each Bhukthi would be 1/12th (0–6–0) of the duration of Mesha Rasi Dasa (6-0-0). The sub-periods in Mesha Rasi Dasa run thus :—

Dasa		*Bhukthi*		*y. m. d.*
Mesha	...	Vrishabha	...	0 6 0
do.	...	Mithuna	...	0 6 0
do.	...	Kataka	...	0 6 0
do.	...	Simha	...	0 6 0
do.	...	Kanya	...	0 6 0
do.	...	Thula	...	0 6 0
do.	...	Vrischika	...	0 6 0
do.	...	Dhanus	...	0 6 0
do.	...	Makara	...	0 6 0
do.	...	Kumbha	...	0 6 0
do.	...	Meena	...	0 6 0
do.	...	Mesha	...	0 6 0
				6 0 0

89. Sthira Dasa

As the name implies, the periods of Sthira Dasa are fixed and they are not variable. Sthira Dasa is held to be very important in determining Maraka or death.

90. Dasa Periods

For purposes of Sthira Dasa calculation, the twelve signs of the Zodiac have been divided into three groups, according to the Chara, Sthira and Dwiswabhava nature of the signs. The durations of the Sthira Dasas of a

Chara Rasi, a Sthira Rasi and a Dwiswabhava Rasi are respectively 7, 8 and 9 years. The following table is self-explanatory:—

Rasi		*Duration of Sthira Dasa*
Mesha	...	7 years
Vrishabha	...	8 "
Mithuna	...	9 "
Kataka	...	7 "
Simha	...	8 "
Kanya	....	9 "
Thula	...	7 "
Vrischika	...	8 "
Dhanus	...	9 "
Makara	...	7 "
Kumbha	...	8 "
Meena	...	9 "
Total	...	96 "

91. Calculation of Sthira Dasa

Two views are expressed as regards the commencement of the Dasa. According to one view, Sthira Dasa starts from Lagna or the 7th whichever is stronger. This view is not supported by Parasara. Jaimini himself is very clear in saying in Sutra * 4 (Adh. II, Pada III) that the Sthira Dasa starts from the Rasi occupied by Brahma) (*see* art. 35). Parasara clearly supports this view. Therefore the first Sthira Dasa starts from the Rasi occupied by Brahma and the subsequent Sthira Dasas succeed in the regular order. There is also a suggestion by some learned men that the balance of the first Sthira Dasa should be found by taking into consideration the degree remaining to be

* Brahmadireva

traversed by the Brahma Graha but this does not seem to have received the approbation of commentators. Some say that if the starting Dasa Rasi is odd, the order of succession would be direct. If it is even, the order would be in the reverse direction.

Example 22

Find the Sthira Dasa periods in the Standard Horoscope.

As Brahma Graha Jupiter is in Aquarius, the 1st Dasa begins from that sign, the duration being 8 years. The next Dasas run in the order of Meena, Mesha, etc., as given below :

	Rasi		*Years*
First Dasa	Kumbha	...	8 0 0
	Meena	...	9 0 0
	Mesha	...	7 0 0
	Vrishabha	...	8 0 0
	Mithuna	...	9 0 0
	Kataka	...	7 0 0
	Simha	...	8 0 0
	Kanya	...	9 0 0
	Thula	...	7 0 0
	Vrischika	...	8 0 0
	Dhanus	....	9 0 0
	Makara	...	7 0 0
			96 0 0

92. Thrikona Dasa

Determine the strongest out of the Lagna, the 5th and the 9th. The first Dasa will start from it. The order of succession will be direct or converse according as the starting Rasi refers to Savya or Apasavya group. If the

1st Dasa Rasi refers to Savya group, then the subsequent Dasa will succeed (in the direct order) in the following manner:—

2nd Dasa	...	5th from 1st
3rd	...	9th
4th	...	2nd
5th	...	6th
6th	...	10th
7th	...	3rd
8th	...	7th
9th	...	11th
10th	...	4th
11th	...	8th
12th	....	12th

Suppose the first Dasa starts from Mithuna. The 2nd Dasa would be that of the 2nd Thrikona (the 5th), the 3rd Dasa, that of Kumbha (9th) the 4th, that of Karkataka (2nd) and so on.

When the first Rasi refers to Apasavya group, then the subsequent Dasas succeed just as mentioned above but in the reverse order. Thus if the 1st Dasa is that of Karkataka, the 3rd Dasa would be that of the 5th from it (counted anti-clockwise), *viz.*, that of Meena, the third that of the 9th (*viz.*, Vrischika), the fourth that of the 2nd (Mithuna) and so on.

93. Span of Thrikona Dasa

The span of a Thrikona Dasa should be ascertained by applying the same method as is done in the case of Chara Dasa, *i.e.*, by counting in the clockwise or anti-clockwise direction (according as Rasi belongs to Savya or Apasavya group) the number of Rasis intervening between the Rasi in question and the lord thereof. Thus if the Dasa period of Cancer is required and the Moon lord is in Simha, Cancer belongs to Apasavya group. Consequently the count must be anti-clockwise. The Moon occupies the 12th (*n*) and therefore the span of the Dasa would be 11 years ($n-1$).

Example 23

Determine the order and duratian of Thrikona Dasas in the Standard and Horoscope.

Out of Lagna, the 5th and 9th, we find the 5th Rasi is the strongest as its numerical strength is 157.5 units (Example 18). The first Thrikona Dasa must therefore start from Kanya. Kanya belongs to Apasavya group, and the order of succession of Dasas is reverse. The span of Dasa periods would be the same as in the case of Chara Dasa, as the undelrying principle is the same. The first Dasa is that of Kanya, the 2nd that of Vrishabha (the 5th from 1st reckoned conversely), the 3rd that of Makara (the 9th), the 4th that of Simha (the 2nd) and reckoning in a similar manner, we could tabulate the Dasas as follows :—

Thrikona Dasas in the Standard Horoscope

Rasi		*Years*
Kanya	...	7 0 0
Vrishabha	...	7 0 0
Makara	...	7 0 0
Simha	...	6 0 0
Mesha	...	6 0 0
Dhanus	. .	2 0 0
Kataka	...	3 0 0
Meena	...	1 0 0
Vrischika	...	11 0 0
Mithuna	...	8 0 0
Kumbha	...	10 0 0
Thula	...	2 0 0

94. Sub-periods in Thrikona Dasa

The duration of a sub-period is one-twelfth of the duration of a major period. The order of succession of sub-periods would be just as the order of succession of Dasas. If the Rasi for which sub-periods are required belongs to Savya group, the sub-periods will succeed in the direct order, the first period being that of the Dasa Rasi, the 2nd being that of the 5th Rasi, the 3rd being that of the 9th Rasi, the 4th being that of the 2nd Rasi, etc., reckoned clockwise. If the Dasa Rasi for which sub-periods are required refers to Apasavya group, then also the above order holds good, but in the reverse direction. Take for instance Cancer. It belongs to Apasavya group. The first sub-period would be that of Cancer, the 2nd would be that of the 5th (counted backwards) *viz.*, Pisces, the 3rd sub-period that of the 9th (counted backwards), *viz.*, Scorpio and so on.

Example 24

Find the sub-periods in the Thrikona Dasas of Dhanus and Makara in the Standard Horoscope.

Dhanus refers to Savya group. The reckoning therefore is in the direct order. The first sub-period would be that of Dhanus, the 2nd that of Mesha (the 5th from the 1st), the 3rd that of Simha, etc., as follows :—

The duration of Dhanus being 2 years each sub-period lasts for 2 months.

Sub-periods in the Thrikona Dasa of Dhanus

Dasa		*Bhukthi*		*y. m. d.*
Dhanus	...	Dhanus	...	0 2 0
Dhanus	...	Mesha	...	0 2 0
do.	...	Simha	...	0 2 0
do.	...	Makara	...	0 2 0
do.	...	Vrishabha	...	0 2 0

Dasa		*Bhukhti*		*y. m. d.*
do.	...	Kanya	...	0 2 0
do.	...	Mithuna	...	0 2 0
do.	..	Kumbha	...	0 2 0
do.	...	Thula	...	0 2 0
do.	...	Meena	...	0 2 0
do.	...	Kataka	...	0 2 0
do.	...	Vrischika	...	0 2 0
		Total	...	2 0 0

Taking the Thrikona Dasa of Makara, the span being 7 years, the duration of each sub-period would be 0-7-0. As Makara balcngs to Apasavya group, the reckoning of sub-periods should be in the reverse order. The first sub-period is that of Makara, the 2nd that of Kanya (the 5th counted backwards from Makara), the 3rd that of Vrishabha and so on as follows:—

Sub-periods in the Thrikona Dasa of Makara

Dasa		*Bhukthi*		*y. m. d*
Makara	...	Makara	...	0 7 0
do.	...	Kanya	..	0 7 0
do.	...	Vrishabha	...	0 7 0
do.	...	Dhanus	...	0 7 0
do.	...	Mesha	...	0 7 0
do.	...	Simha	...	0 7 0
do.	...	Vrischika	..	0 7 0
do.	...	Kataka	...	0 7 0
do.	...	Meena	..	0 7 0
do.	...	Thula	...	0 7 0
do.	...	Mithuna	..	0 7 0
do.	...	Kumbha	..	0 7 0
		Total		7 0 0

95. Varnada Dasa

This is based upon the relationship between Lagna and the Varnada Lagna. We have already explained in article 22 how to calculate Varnada Lagna. In the same manner, Varnadas for the 2nd, 3rd and other Bhavas should be calculated. If the Lagna is odd, the order of Dasa would be direct; if even, reverse. Different commentators have expressed different opinions as to the starting and reckoning of Varnada Dasa and I do not propose to deal with these controversial matters in a book mainly intended for the students of astrology. According to some, the Dasa must start either from Lagna or from Hora Lagna whichever is stronger. I take my clue from Sutra 16 of Pada 3 of Adhyaya IV in which Jaimini suggests that Varnada Dasa should commence from Lagna and run in the direct order if Lagna is an odd sign, and from the 12th and run in the reverse order, if Lagna is an even sign. The counting of the Dasa should also be direct or otherwise depending upon the odd or even nature of the rising sign. Thus if Lagna is Mesha and the Varnada Lagna is Kanya, then the 1st Varnada Dasa would be that of Mesha and its duration would be 6 years, the distance counted clockwise from Lagna to Varnada Lagna. If, on the other hand, the Lagna were to be Vrishabha and Varnada Lagna Kanya, then the first Varnada Dasa would be that of Mesha, its duration being 8 years the distance from the 12th from Lagna to Varnada Lagna, counted backwards. The 2nd Varnada Dasa, in the case of an odd sign, would be that of the second Rasi, its duration being equivalent to the distance between Lagna and the 2nd Varnada Rasi reckoned directly. In case Lagna is an even sign, the 2nd Dasa would be that of 3rd Rasi from Lagna or the 2nd

Rasi from 12th (counted in the anti-clockwise direction) the duration being the distance in terms of signs betwee the Lagna and 2nd Varnada counted in the reverse order

Summing up, when Lagna is odd, the order of Dasa would be direct. The span of a Varnada Dasa would be the interval between Lagna and the Varnada concerned in the direct order when the Lagna is odd. When the Lagna is even, the order would be converse and the duration of Varnada Dasa would be equivalent to the internal between the 12th (from Lagna) and the Varnada in question counted backwards.

Example 25

Determine a few Varnada Dasas in the Standard Horoscope.

Example 5 gives the Varnada Lagna as Sagittarius and 2nd Varnada—as Vrishabha. Since Janma Lagna is even, the order of Dasa is converse and the counting will be from the 12th, *i.e.,* Mesha. The first Varnada Dasa is that of Mesha (the 12th from Vrishabha). Counting from the 12th from Janma Lagna to Varanda (in the reverse order) we get 5 as the span of Varnada Dasa. Similarly, the 2nd Dasa will be that of Meena. The 2nd Varnada is Vrishabha. Counting from the 12th from Janma Lagna to Vrishabha, the sign of 2nd Varnada we get 12 as the duration of Meena Varnada.

∴ Mesha Varnada	—	—	5 0 0
Meena Varnada	—	—	12 0 0

96. Brahma Dasa

If Lagna is odd, then the Dasa commences from Brahma Rasi and the order of succession is direct. If Lagna is even the Dasa commences from the 7th from Brahma Rasi and the order of succession is in the reverse order. The span of a Dasa, irrespective of the order of succession being direct or indirect, is equivalent to the number of Rasis intervening between the Rasi in question and the Rasi where the 6th lord from the concerned Rasi is situated. In case where Lagna is Mesha and Brahma is in Vrischika, Mars occupying Kanya, the succession of Dasas would be direct from Brahma Rasi, as the Lagna is odd. As the 6th lord from Vrischika, the starting Dasa, is the 11th from Vrischika, the span of Vrischika Dasa would be 11—1 = 10 years.

The distinction between Sthira Dasa and Brahma Dasa is that in the former scheme, the periods are fixed, though commencing from Brahma, while the latter no doubt commences from Brahma or the 7th from it, but the periods are variable.

Example 26

Find the Brahma Dasas in the Standard Horoscope.

T he agna is Vrishabha an even sign. Brahma is in Kumbha. Therefore the first Brahma Dasa commences from Simha (the 7th from Brahma) and runs in the anti-clockwise order, *viz.*, Simha, Kataka, etc. The 6th lord from Simha, *viz.*, Sani is in the 11th from Simha. Hence the period of Simha Dasa is (11—1) = 10 years. The lord of the 6th from the next Dasa Rasi, *viz.*, Jupiter is in the 8th from Cancer. Hence the Dasa of Karkataka extends for 7 years. Similarly considered for other Rasis, we get the following spans :—

Brahma Dasas in the Standard Horoscope

Simha	...	10 0 0
Karkataka	...	7 0 0
Mithuna	...	4 0 0
Vrishabha	...	7 0 0
Mesha	...	10 0 0

Meena	...	11 0 0
Kumbha	...	2 0 0
Makara	...	1 0 0
Dhanus	...	12 0 0
Vrischika	...	11 0 0
Thula	...	4 0 0
Kanya	.	9 0 0

Some are of opinion that in the counting of the span, direct and reverse order should be followed according as the Lagna is odd or even.

97. Yogardha Dasa

The first Dasa starts from the Lagna or the 7th whichever is stronger. The order of Dasa succession would be direct or converse according as the Rasi of the starting Dasa is odd or even. The duration of the Yogardha Dasa of a Rasi is half the sum of its Chara and Sthira Dasa periods.

Example 27

Find the order and duration of Yogardha Dasas in the Standard Horoscope.

Of the Lagna and the 7th, Lagna is stronger because Vrishabha's total strength is more than that of Vrischika. Therefore the first Yogardha Dasa would be that of Vrishabha. As the Rasi of the 1st Dasa is even, the order of succession would be reverse, *vi.*, Vrishabha, Mesha, etc. The duration of Vrishabha Yogardha Dasa is $\frac{1}{2}$ (Chara Dasa of Vrishabha + Sthira Dasa of Vrishabha).

$\frac{1}{2}$(Yrs. 7—0—0 + 8—0—0) = $7\frac{1}{2}$ years.

Similarly reckoned, the following are the Yogardha Dasas and their duration :—

		y. m. d.
Vrishabha	...	7 6 0
Mesha	...	6 6 0
Meena	...	5 0 0
Kumbha	..	9 0 0
Makara	...	7 0 0
Dhanus	...	5 6 0
Vrischika	...	9 6 0
Thula	...	4 6 0
Kanya	...	8 0 0
Simha	...	7 0 0
Karkataka	...	5 0 0
Mithuna	....	8 6 0
		83 0 0

Some scholars hold that in case of women, the Dasa must always commence from the 7th irrespective of whether Lagna or the 7th is stronger.

98. Niryana Sula Dasa

Considerable importance is given to this system of Dasa by students of Jaimini Astrology. Explanations by commentators are vague as to the method and scope of calculating Niryana Sula Dasa. I am therefore giving the most popular method. If the Lagna is an odd sign, the Dasa must start from Lagna. If the Lagna is an even sign, the Dasa starts from the 7th. The order is direct or converse according as the Lagna is odd or even. The duration of each Dasa is 9 years.

Example 28

Calculate Niryana Sula Dasa in the Standard Horoscope.

The Lagna Taurus is even.

The Dasa must start from the 7th, *viz.*, Vrischika and run in the reverse order, *viz.*, Thula, etc. The span of Dasa is 9 years. The following is the order, etc. :—

Vrischika	...	9 0 0
Thula	...	9 0 0
Kanya	...	9 0 0
Simha	...	9 0 0
Kataka	...	9 0 0
Mithuna	...	9 0 0
Vrishabha	...	9 0 0
Mesha	...	9 0 0
Meena	...	9 0 0
Kumbha	...	9 0 0
Makara	...	9 0 0
Dhanus	...	9 0 0
Total	...	108 0 0

99. Niryana Phala Sula Dasa

This is employed mostly for predicting the native's death. The duration of each Dasa is 9 years, It starts from the 7th from Maraka Rasi and succeeds directly or conversely according as Lagna is odd or even and Maraka is said to happen when the Dasa reaches the Maraka Rasi, which it generally does when the age is from 54 to 63. Hence in actual practice it cannot be applied to Purnayu horoscopes.

100. Other Dasas

There are quite a number of Dasas dealt with by Jaimini such as Manduka Dasa, Nakshatra Dasa, Shula Dasa, Drug Dasa, etc., which I do not propose to deal with in the course of these *Studies*. Parasara has given a number of Dasas but only two, *viz.*, Vimshottari and Ashtottari are in vogue. Even out of these two, the most popular is of course the Vimshottari. Similarly with regard to Jaimini, even though the Sage deals with a number of Dasas, sometimes casually hinting that a particular Dasa system should be applied for making predictions pertaining to a particular Bhava, Chara Dasa, Thrikona Dasa and Sthira Dasa, when properly studied and understood, should enable us to predict almost all events. It is for students with an investigative bent of mind to apply the various Dasas and pick out the best and the most satisfactory one.

CHAPTER VI

Determination of Longevity

101. General Observations

Longevity determination has always been a hard nut to crack. Several methods, predictive as well as mathematical, are in vogue but the mathematical methods seem to hardly work in actual practice. Of the predictive methods, rules for Maraka determination *plus* the Gochara dispositions would enable one to anticipate the probable duration of life fairly accurately.

102. Jaimini's Methods

Jaimini has given a number of combinations for predicting longevity, the rules being scattered in different chapters seemingly lacking continuity of presentation and consequently leading a student to confusion. In these pages, I have confined myself to the discussion of just those principles, which, in my humble opinion, could be safely relied upon for accuracy. It is superfluous for me to remind readers that these *Studies* are not a literal presentation of all the Jaiminian principles but a summary of the essentials which I have had the occasion to test with considerable satisfaction. The various methods suggested by Jaimini have been grouped by me into three kinds which for the sake of convenience, I would call A, B and C.

103. Terms of Longevity

All astrological writers divide the span of human life into three distinct categories, *viz.*, Alpa, Madhya and Deergha or short life, middle life and long life respectively. But the terms allotted vary with regard to different authors. But the most commonly accepted terms for purposes of application of Jaimini are: Alpayu upto 32 years, Madhyayu 33 to 64 years and Deerghayu 65 to 100 years.

104. Method One

Three sets of two factors each are employed for ascertaining longevity. They are :—(*a*) Lords of Lagna and 8th, (*b*) Lagna and the Moon and (*c*) Lagna and Hora Lagna.

105. Alpayu

Short life is indicated if out of two factors of a set (art. 104) one is in Chara and the other is in Dwiswabhava, (*b*) if both are in Sthira, (*c*) and if one is in Dwiswabhava and the other is in Chara. The reckoning should be made in respect of all the three sets of factors. The term of longevity for Alpayu is 32 years.

106. Madhyayu

Middle life or Madhyayu is indicated if out of the two factors (*a*) one is in Chara and the other is in Sthira, (*b*) one in Sthira and the other in Chara or (*c*) both in Dwiswabhava. The reckoning should be made in respect of all the three sets of factors. The term of Madhyayu is 64 years.

107. Purnayu

This is caused, if of the two factors (*a*) both are in Chara, (*b*) one is in Sthira and the other in Dwiswabhava, and (*c*) one in Dwiswabhava and the other in Sthira. The reckoning should be made in respect of all the three sets of factors. The term of Purnayu is considered to be 130 by some and 120 by others. But we propose to consider 100 years for purposes of illustrating Jaimini's principles.

108. Reconciling Contradictory Results

If two or all the three sets of factors reveal the same term of life, then it must be accepted. If each set reveals different terms, then preference should be given to the term of life denoted by Lagna and Hora Lagna. If, however, when three different terms are obtained, and the Moon is in Lagna or the 7th, the term of longevity indicated by Lagna and the Moon should be preferred. Call the longevity obtained according to this method as A.

109. Calculation of Exact Longevity

After ascertaining the term of life—Alpayu, Madhyayu or Purnayu—to which a particular nativity belongs, the exact number of years can be calculated thus. If supposing Madhyayu is indicated ; the full term of 66 years is granted, provided the lords of Lagna and the 8th are at the beginning of the respective signs occupied by them. If however they happen to be in the last degree of the Rasis concerned, they give zero years in the term and death may take place at the close of Alpayu. If they are in the intermediate positions, the years given by them should be ascertained separately by rule of three. The sum of the years given by the two factors (lords of Lagna and the 8th) divided by 2 would be the actual number of years gained in that particular category of Ayurdaya or longevity.

Suppose Purnayu is indicated and the lords of Lagna and the 8th are in 25° and 12° respectively in the respective signs occupied by them. The lord of Lagna is removed from the first point of the sign by 25° and at the rate of 1·1 year per degree the reduction due to his position would be $25 \times 1{\cdot}1 = 27{\cdot}5$ years. This is as good as saying that he will give 5·5 (33—27·5) years as his quota in the term of Purnayu. Similarly, the lord of the 8th, having been removed from the beginning of the sign concerned by 12°, the reduction due would be $12 \times 1{\cdot}1 = 13{\cdot}2$ years. Or the 8th lord gives 19·8 (33—13·2) years as his quota. The actual quota given by these two lords is the mean of the sum of the years separately given. Here the actual quota would be $\frac{19{\cdot}8 + 5{\cdot}5}{2} = 12{\cdot}65$ years. This must be added to 66 from which Purnayu starts and total length of life would be $66 + 12{\cdot}65 = 78{\cdot}65$ years.

110. Summary

The following formulae facilitate calculation of the exact period of longevity :—

Alpayu : $(3°—x) = 1{\cdot}1$

Madhyayu : $a + (30—x) = 1{\cdot}1$

Purnayu : $b + (30—x) = 1{\cdot}1$

(where x = Long. of the planet devoid of signs, a = term of Alpayu and b = term of Madhyayu).

111. Method Two

(*a*) Find out the stronger of the lords of the 8th from Lagna and the 8th from the 7th. According as the lord is in a Kendra, Panapara or Apoklima, the term of life would be long, medium or short. Call the longevity obtained according to this method as B.

112. Method Three

Apply the above rules in respect of the stronger of the lords of the 8th from Atmakaraka and the 8th from the 7th from Atmakaraka and ascertain the term of life. Call the longevity obtained as C. If, however, the Atmakaraka occupies the 9th from Lagna, Alpayu becomes Purnayu and *vice versa* but Madhyayu remains as such.

There is a suggestion in III, Pada 2, that in determining longevity, the Lagna and Atmakaraka should also be considered in the same manner as Lagna and Chandra.

113. Observations

As in Parasari, quite a number of methods are given by Jaimini for ascertaining longevity. There is no hint anywhere as to the suitability or otherwise of any particular method under any particular horoscopic conditions. It occurs to me therefore that from a practical point of view, the following procedure may be adopted.

Find out the terms of life according to A, B and C, and declare that term which is revealed by the majority of considerations. Thus if *Method One* reveals Alpayu, *Method Two* reveals Madhyayu and *Method Three* Madhyayu, say the native has Madhyayu. If methods 1, 2 and 3 reveal different terms, then assign A, B or C according as the Hora Lagna, Lagna or Atmakaraka is the strongest.

114. Kaksha Vriddhi

This means the increase of term of longevity, Alpayu becoming Madhyayu, and Madhyayu becoming Purnayu.

115. Conditions for Kaksha Vriddhi

There will be Kaksha Vriddhi when any one of the following conditions are present. (*a*) The Lagna and the 7th have been hemmed in between benefics. (*b*) Atmakaraka and the 7th from Atmakaraka are hemmed in between benefics. (*c*) When benefics are present in Lagna or the 7th or in a Trikona from them. (*d*) When benefics are with Atmakaraka, or in the Trikonas from him. (*e*) When the Atmakaraka being a benefic is not debilitated but is exalted or is with malefics. (*f*) When Guru has benefics on either side, or in Trikonas. (*g*) When Jupiter is in Lagna or the 7th, devoid of malefic aspects or associations.

116. Kaksha Hrasa

This means a particular term of longevity being reduced to the next lower one, thus Purnayu becoming Madhyayu and Madhyayu becoming Alpayu.

117. Conditions for Kaksha Hrasa

There will be Kaksha Hrasa, (*a*) when either the 8th lord from Lagna or the 8th lord from the 7th becomes or joins the Atmakaraka, (*b*) when Lagna and the 7th are hemmed in between malefics or have malefics disposed in Trikonas, (*c*) when Atmakaraka or the 7th from Atmakaraka is between malefics or has malefics disposed in Trines, and (*d*) when Atmakaraka being a malefic is debilitated or associated with malefics.

118. Rasi Vriddhi

This means increase of longevity by a Rasi. If the places suggested for benefics for Kaksha Vriddhi in art. 115 are occupied by Full Moon or Venus, then there will be increase of longevity by one Rasi Dasa.

119. Rasi Hrasa

This means the decrease of longevity by one Rasi Dasa. Rasi Hrasa will be caused when Sani occupies the places suggested for malefics for Kaksha Hrasa.

Example 29

Find out the longevity in the Standard Horoscope.

Method 1:

(*i*) Lords of Lagna and 8th are in Dwiswabhava and Sthira ; hence Purnayu.

(*ii*) Lagna and the Moon are in Sthira and Chara—Madhyayu.

(*iii*) Lagna and Hora Lagna are Sthira and Chara—Madhyayu.

∵ the same term, *viz.*, Madhyayu by two sets of factors is indicated, accept it.

The horoscope belongs to Madhyayu category : (A).

Method 2 :

Lord of 8th from Lagna is Jupiter.

Lord of 8th from 7th is Mercury.

Jupiter is more powerful than Mercury according to Rasi Bala.

Jupiter occupies a Kendra.

∴ Term of Life = Purnayu : (B).

Method 3 :

Lord of 8th from Atmakaraka is Mercury.

Lord of 8th from the 7th from Atmakaraka—Jupiter.

Jupiter is more powerful than Mercury.

Jupiter himself is Atmakaraka and is in a Kendra from Lagna.

∴ Term of Life—Purnayu : (C).

Atmakaraka is not in the 9th from Lagna. Hence no further correction is necessary.

∵ The horoscope belongs to the category of Purnayu as rvealed by 2 and 3.

∴ There is neither Kaksha Vriddhi nor Kaksha Hrasa because factors for and against counterbalance each other.

For Vriddhi :—(*a*) Atmakaraka is a benefic.
(*b*) Atmakaraka is Guru himself,

Far Hrasa :—(*a*) The 8th lord from Lagna is Atmakaraka.
(*b*) Lagna and 7th hemmed in between malefics.

120. Remarks

In applying the various methods of longevity determination, due attention should necessarily be paid to the general strength of the horoscope. Mark for instance the strong disposition of Atmakaraka in the Standard Horoscope. He is in Kendra from Lagna and is the strongest planet in the horoscope because of the strength of the Rasi he is in. When the Atmakaraka is so strongly posited, no matter, whatever be the other factors, the native will have full life.

121. The Main Period of Death

A number of combinations have been mentioned for predicting the probable time of death. Some scholars are of opinion that any of the Dasas mentioned by Jaimini could be applied provided one is thorough with the technique. Still others hold that only Shula Dasa should be made use of for predicting death. There is also a school of thought according to which Navamsa Dasa and Sthira Dasa should alone be employed for purposes of ascertaining Maraka period. It is our personal view, and this may be taken for what it is worth, that in determining Maraka, Sthira Dasa and Shula Dasa may be tried with fair chances of success. I give below some select principles bearing on Maraka determination.

(*a*) If the 7th from Atmakaraka or Lagna is occupied by Saturn, Rahu or Ketu, death occurs in the 1st, 2nd or 3rd part of the divisions concerned. That is when the term of life is Madhya, and the 7th is occupied by Sani, death can happen in the 1st part of Madhyayu; if Rahu is in the 7th, in the 2nd part of Madhyayu; if Ketu is in the 7th, in the third part. This principle is applicable to all the three terms.

(*b*) Death is likely in the Dasas of Rasis which happen to be Trikonas to the 8th house.

(*c*) When Saturn is in the 8th, death may be anticipated in the Dasa of the 8th Rasi. Here the reference is to the Navamsa Dasa.

(*d*) If the 8th Rasi has mixed influences, *i.e.*, of benefics as well as of malefics, death is likely in the Dasa of the 8th Rasi.

(*e*) Death happens in the Dasa of a death-inflicting Rasi (in Sthira Dasa) provided the said Dasa falls within the terms of life fixed for the native. Thus if a person has Purnayu and the death-inflicting Rasi Dasa rules before commencement of Purnayu term, then death does not take place.

(*f*) Death is also possible in the Dasa of a Rasi (*i*) that is hemmed in between malefics; and (*ii*) that has malefics disposed in the 8th and 12th from it.

(*g*) Death may happen in the Dasa of the 8th or 12th Rasi provided it is devoid of aspects of planets other than weak Moon and Venus.

(*h*) If malefics or Rudra is in the 8th or 2nd from Lagna, Moon or Atmakaraka, death takes place in the Dasa of the Rasi previous to the Dasa of the death-inflicting Rasi.

(*i*) Death is also possible in the Dasa of the 8th Rasi from the Sun and Venus.

(*j*) Longevity generally extends from Brahma to Maheswara (according to Sthira Dasa).

(*k*) Death is also likely in the Dasa of the Rasi held by Rudra.

(*l*) Death can also take place in the Dasa (according to Sthira Dasa reckoning) of the Rasi occupied by Maheswara, and in the Antardasas of 1st, 5th and 9th Rasis from the Rasi held by the lord of 8th from Maheswara.

(*m*) The strongest of the lord of the 3rd, 6th, 8th and 12th from Atmakaraka becomes the maraka and death takes place in the Dasa of the Rasi held by him.

(*n*) When two or three lords as per above become marakas, choose the one whose Rasi Dasa (*i.e.*, the Dasa of the Rasi occupied by him) is appropriate to the terms of life. That is, if supposing three Rasis become marakas, all being equal in strength. The native has Purnayu. Suppose the Dasa of 2 planets come before Purnayu and that of other during the course of Purnayu. Then the Maraka will be the Rasi whose Dasa falls within the Purnayu span.

122. The Sub-period of Death

(*a*) In the course of a Maraka Dasa, death can be brought about in the sub-Dasa of the strongest of the lord of 6th, 2nd and 12th from Atmakaraka, *i.e.*, in the sub-period of the Rasi held by such planet.

(*b*) In the Rasi occupied by Rudra.

(*c*) In the minor periods of the Navamsa Rasis held by lord of Maraka Rasi and the 6th therefrom.

Suppose Maraka Rasi is Cancer. The lord of this, and that of the 6th from it are the Moon and Jupiter respectively. Suppose they are in Meena and Thula

Navamsas respectively. Then in the Maraka Dasa concerned, death can happen in the sub-periods of Meena and Thula.

123. Certain Exceptions

When the Dwara and Bahya Rasis are afflicted, death takes place in their own Navamsa Dasa.

When the 8th lord from Lagna is exalted, there will be a gain of one Navamsa Rasi Dasa, *i.e.*, 9 years. In such a circumstance, death takes place in Navamsa Dasa of Rasis, which are in a trikona from lords of Lagna and 8th or in the Navamsa Dasa of the Rasi occupied by the lord.

Example 30

Determine the Maraka Rasi in the Standard Horoscope.

Applying the principles given in articles 121 and 122.

(*b*) The Trikona Rasis to 8th house are Dhanus, Mesha and Simha. Death is likely in the Dasa of the strongest of the three Rasis, *viz.*, Dhanus (*vide*. Ex 18).

(*f*) Taurus is hemmed in between malefics. Hence Taurus is also a death inflicting Rasi.

Dhanus has a malefic disposed in the 8th. Hence it is a death-inflicting Rasi.

(*g*) Death may happen in the Dasa of Dhanus (8th Rasi) or Aries (12th Rasi) but as Aries is not devoid of aspects of planets other than weak Moon and Venus (*i.e.*, is aspected by Jupiter, Sun and Mercury) it cannot cause Maraka.

Dhanus is dovoid of aspects (except that of Saturn) but is associated with Venus. Hence it acquires Maraka power.

(*i*) Kanya and Kataka are also death-inflicting Rasis.

(*k*) Kumbha also can cause death as it is the Rasi occupied by Rudra and Meheswara.

(*m*) The strongest out of the lords of the 3rd (Mars), 6th (Moon), 8th (Mercury) and 12th (Saturn) from Atmakaraka is Mercury (*vide* Ex. 16). He occupies Kumbha. Therefore Kumbha can become a maraka sign.

Thus the following Rasis have acquired death-inflicting power :—

(*b*) Dhanus.
(*f*) Vrishabha, Dhanus.
(*g*) Dhanus.
(*i*) Kanya and Kataka.
(*k*) Kumbha.
(*m*) Kumbha.

Dhanus becomes by far the most powerful Rasi capable of causing death in its Dasa. As regards the sub-period (*vide* article 122) the strongest of the lords of 6th (Moon), 2nd (Jupiter) and the 12th (Saturn) from Atmakaraka is Jupiter. Hence during the sub-Dasa of Kumbha (the sign occupied by Jupiter) in the Maha Dasa of Dhanus (as per Sthira Dasa reckoning) death is likely.

Dhanus Dasa (Sthira Dasa) commences from the 81st year of the native and Kumbha Bhukthi starts when the native is aged 81 years 6 months. He died in his 82nd year.

CHAPTER VII

Judgment of Horoscope

124. Preliminary Remarks

The crux of the problem in astrology is horoscope-judgment. Jaimini's approach in this regard is quite unique. I have collected combinations bearing on the different Bhavas scattered in different Adhyayas.

125. Karakamsa

We have already seen in article 8 that Atmakaraka is the planet who gets the highest number of degrees in a sign. Karakamsa is the Navamsa occupied by Atmakaraka.

126. Physical Appearance

Though there does not appear to be any suggestion anywhere in Jaimini's Sutras that the sign rising at birth determines the personal appearance and character of the person concerned, yet we have to give due consideration to the sign factor. The physical features, complexion, etc., are to be known by the nature of Karakamsa lord, the Navamsa lord and Varnada Lagna, the last being specially important for judging the complexion. Planets rising in the Lagna, Navamsa Lagna, Varnada Lagna and in Karakamsa impart to the person their respective characteristics.

* Colours of the planets are to be taken as suggested in the general astrological principles. When in Lagna, Navamsa Lagna, Karakamsa or Varnada, Ketu and Saturn conjoin, the complexion would be light red; Rahu and Suturn—dark; Saturn and Venus—blackish; Saturn and Jupiter—golden colour; Saturn and Mercury—bluish; Saturn and Mars—Raktasuvarna or reddish yellow; and Saturn and the Moon—white.

Pranapada (art. 30) falling in Kanya gives ruddiness to the complexion and produces softness and greater delicacy; in Makara—fairly ruddish complexion; Simha—ugly. The person looks as though aged if Ketu occupies the 2nd from Lagnarudha (art. 19). Saturn in the 2nd from the lord of the 7th from Upapada** makes one's appearance extremely uncouth or ugly. Mercury and Venus in the 2nd or 5th give ugly jaws and lips.

Example 31

Judge the physical appearance of the native in the Standard Horoscope.

The lord of Lagna is Sukra, Karakamsa lord is Mars, Navamsa Lagna lord is Mars, Varnada Lagna lord is Sukra. As Mars and Venus are the dominant planets, the native partakes of the characteristics of Mars and Venus, *viz.*, fair complexion, healthy constitution, large eyes, dignified stature and softness and delicacy.

127. Character and Mind

Pranapada Lagna falling in Kumbha will make the subject a hypocrite. He will be depressed and gloomy if

* The Sun to Saturn represent red, white, reddish, green, yellow, mixed and black colours respectively. 11.3 *Brihat Jataka.*

** Upapada is the "Arudha Rasi" of the 12th from Lagna; in other words find out the "Arudha" for the 12th house as per Art. 19.

the Moon and Rahu are in the 5th or aspect the 5th. He will be wicked and of destructive nature if Moon and Rahu are in the 9th from Lagna or Atmakaraka. The Lagna being aspected by Mars is co-existent with a quick, wrathful and passionate temperament. An inspirational and righteous nature is revealed if Karakamsa happens to fall in Meena. The person commits sinful deeds and becomes a hypocrite if Ketu joins Karakamsa, while the Sun and Rahu in Karakamsa aspected by Mars confers a destructive temperament. One becomes firm-minded if the 10th from Karakamsa is not joined by Mercury but is aspected by other benefics. Malefics in the 3rd from Karakamsa make one brave. If the 5th and 9th from Karakamsa are occupied by malefics but aspected by benefics, one possesses generous instincts. Saturn in Karakamsa or in the 5th from it indicates great nervousness in assemblies. One lacks power of expression, or will be an indistinct speaker if the 2nd from Karakamsa is occupied by Ketu and aspected by malefics. The subject will be highly intelligent, if the 5th lord aspects Atmakaraka or Lagna. One will lead a happy life if the 4th lord from Lagna (or Atmakaraka) aspects the Lagna (or Atmakaraka). Lord of the 12th from Lagna (or Atmakaraka) aspecting Lagna (or Atmakaraka) makes one a spendthrift.

Example 32

Judge the mental characteristics in the Standard Horoscope.

The Lagna is aspected by Mars—a quick and passionate temperament. The 5th lord Mercury is with Atmakaraka—the native was a man of precocious inteligence. He led a happy life because the 4th lord from Lagna, *viz.*, Sun has joined the Atmakaraka. The native was noted for his character. He was of sweet manners, forgiving temperament and found of progressive and responsible movements. Mark the disposition of Lagnadhipathi in the sign of Atmakaraka and Karakamsa being strongly disposed and the 5th lord Mercury joining Atmakaraka.

128. Financial Prospects

By the general strength of the horoscope and by applying the usual principles of astrology, one's financial worth is to be judged.

The 11th from Lagnarudha being occupied by exalted or friendly planets gives rise to immense wealth. The earnings would be through legitimate or questionable means according as the planet or planets in the 11th are good or evil. If Arudha Lagna is associated with or aspected by benefics, the native becomes wealthy. There will be considerable wealth if the 2nd from Lagnarudha is occupied by Venus, Moon and Jupiter. If the Arudha Rasi of the 7th house happens to be a kendra, kona or the 3rd or 11th from Lagnarudha, the person earns a lot of money and amasses good fortune. Arudha Rasi of the 7th falling in the 6th, 8th or 12th from Lagnarudha will produce difficulty in acquiring money and there will be great poverty. Immense wealth will be conferred if the Lagnarudha (or Lagna) and the Arudha of the 7th house (or 7th house) are not subject to malefic argalas (see art. 45 & 46) or have benefic argalas. Poverty will result if the lord of the 8th from Atmakaraka (or Lagna) aspects the Atmakaraka (or Lagna).

There will be destruction of wealth through association with women of ill-repute if the 9th from Karakamasa is joined by Rahu. The 2nd house from Lagnarudha being joined or aspected by benefics or by the lord of Lagnarudha or Yogakaraka planets (see art. 140) confers good financial prospects. The best combination for financial prosperity is an aspect or association between the Atmakaraka (or the lord of Atmakaraka sign) and the 2nd lord from Atmakaraka.

Example 33

Judge the financial Prospects in the Standard Horoscope.

Lagnarudha, *viz.*, Cancer has the argala of Mars, but it is counteracted by the presence of Moon in the 10th. The argala caused to Lagna by Sani is neutralised by the presence of Chandra and Rahu in the 12th The 7th house is subjected to benefic argalas and there is no counteraction of these argalas. The 2nd from Lagnarudha is aspected by the Moon (and also Rahu) lord of Lagnarudha. The 2nd house from Atmakaraka is aspected by Sani lord of Atmakaraka sign. Consequently the subject's financial conditions were very good. Mark the fact that Arudha Lagna has the aspect of jupiter, Atmakaraka and a natural benefic and that of the Sun lord of the 2nd from Arudha Lagna. Mark also the fact that Arudha of the 7th falls in the 3rd from Lagnarudha. The person earned a lot. Budha, the lord of the 8th from Atmakaraka, is with Atmakaraka. This perhaps accounts for his having spent away all his earnings.

129. Health and Disease

The person will be generally healthy if the 8th house is aspected by the lord of the 9th. The organs represented by the zodiacal signs ruling them will be developed or otherwise according as the signs concerned are conjoined with or aspected by benefics or malefics. According to Jaimini, the Lagna and the other bhavas in regular order typify respectively the head, face, neck, arms, stomach, shanks (jaghanam), buttocks (prishta), sexual organs, legs, eyes and ears. The Sun or Lagna whichever is stronger, denotes the deha or body. The Moon or Lagna, whichever is stronger, denotes the heart. If Pitrukaraka and Matrukaraka are before *deha* defects in the constitution arise late in life. The situation of the Atmakaraka in a particular Navamsa (Karakamsa) is said to predispose the subject to certain troubles and dangers. The results of the location of Atmakaraka in the different Navamsas are as follows :—

Aries :—Fear from cats, rats and similar creatures. *Taurus* :—Bulls, horses and similar quadrupes. *Gemini*—Frequent suffering from cutaneous diseases and an inclination towards corpulence. *Cancer* :—Dangers from aquatic sources and diseases like leprosy. *Leo* :—Fear from dogs and other canine animals *Virgo* :—Danger from fire, skin troubles and inclination towards corpulence. *Scorpio* :--Fear from animals, insects and reptiles, *Sagittarius* :—Accidents from conveyances, falls from high places. *Capricorn* :—Troubles from fishes, whales, wild animals, women and spirits. *Aquarius* :—Mental disturbances, Insomnia: *Pisces* :—Watery disease, particularly dropsy and swelling of feet.

The subject will be generally healthy if the Atmakaraka is free from malefic associations and aspects. If the Moon is in Karakamsa aspected by Mars, the person suffers from complicated diseases. The following special combinations indicate the diseases one is likely to suffer from. The severity of the disease must be judged from the strength of the afflicted planets and the amount of relief given by good aspects.

(*a*) Swelling of Testicles or Hernia :—Karakamsa in association with Gulika and aspected by Mercury.

(*b*) Ear troubles :—Karakamsa joined by Ketu and aspected by or associated with malefics.

(*c*) White leprosy :—The Moon in the 4th from Karakamsa aspected by Venus.

(*d*) Black leprosy :—The Moon in the 4th from Karakamsa aspected by Ketu.

(*e*) Consumption :—Mars and Rahu in the 4th or 5th from Karakamsa disposes one to consumption. If the Moon aspects Mars, the disease becomes incurable.

(*f*) Tumours and abscesses are caused by the presence of Mars in the 4th from Karakamsa: or there will be eruptions, boils or skin diseases.

(*g*) Dropsy : Ketu in the 4th from Karakamsa.

(*h*) Gastric troubles are caused if Rahu or Ketu is in the 7th from Lagnarudha. The most important factors are the Lagna, the sign occupied by Atmakaraka and Karakamsa and the 6th from these places. In general, afflictions to the 6th from Atmakaraka Rasi and Karakamsa produce more serious consequences than those to the 6th from Lagna. The relative affliction possessed by the 6th house from each of the above factors should be taken into consideration.

Example 34

Judge the nature of health of the native in the Standard Horoscope.

The 8th house is aspected by Saturn lord of the 9th. The native was generally healthy. The 6th from Karakamsa is occupied by Moon and the 5th lord from Karakamsa is in a benefic sign. Again the 6th from Atmakaraka has the aspects of Mercury and Atmakaraka Jupiter. The native never suffered from any serious disease or ill-health. The 9th from Atmakaraka is occupied by two malefics Kuja and Ketu. The 9th rules feet. It was during Thula Dasa (Sthira) that his left foot became slightly swollen and this remained practically till his death.

130. Educational Prospects

According to Parasara, education is generally ascertained from the 4th house. Jaimini's treatment of the subject bearing on education is not exhaustive. He gives a few combinations for proficiency in different branches of knowledge. It is for readers to put these principles into such use as they deem fit. Jupiter in Karakamsa or in the 5th from it gives proficiency in grammar, Vedas and Vedangas. Mercury in Karakamsa or 5th from it indicates a good insight into Meemamsa. Mars in Karakamsa or in the 5th from it gives high legal education. When the Moon is in Karakamsa or in the 5th from it, it makes one a musician or gives him scholarship in literature. Ketu in Karakamsa or in the 5th from it gives proficieney in mathematics. When the above combinations are aspected by Jupiter, the person becomes a versatile genius.

Example 35

Indicate the educational prospects in the Standard Horoscope.

The 5th from Karakamsa is occupied by Moon and aspected by Budha. The subject possessed great scholarship in literature and was a lover of music. Mark also the association of the 5th lord Mercury with Atmakaraka. Judged from Parasara's methods, the house of education is strongly fortified by being aspected by the lords of the 4th, 5th and Jupiter.

131. Parents

The general significators the Pitrukaraka and Matrukaraka are determined as per article 11. The good disposition of the 4th from Arudha Lagna and the Matrukaraka is necessary for getting a good and long-lived mother. The father will be long-lived if the Pitrukaraka and the 9th from Arudha Lagna are not afflicted.

132. Brothers and Sisters

The third house from Upapada rules younger brothers and sisters and the eleventh house from Upapada rules elder brothers and sisters. There will be death of brothers if the 3rd or 11th from Upapada Lagna (or lord of Upapada) are occupied by Rahu and Sani.

The mother will have abortions if the 3rd or 11th from Upapada or its lord is occupied by Venus. The person will have a number of brothers and sisters if Mars, Jupiter and the Moon are in the 11th and 3rd houses from Upapada or its lord. The elder brother will die if the 11th from Upapada or its lord is aspected by Saturn and Mars. If the house afflicted is the 3rd, then the younger brother will die. Mars in the 11th or 3rd from Upapada or its lord, aspected by Saturn, will cause the death of all brothers, excepting the native. The person will have elder or younger sisters according as the 11th or 3rd from Upapada is occupied by its lord or Ketu.

No clue is given for ascertaining the actual number of brothers and sisters. Obviously we have to fall on the general principles and judge the number taking into consideration the navamsas gained by the 3rd and 11th bhavas or Bhratrukaraka.

Example 36

Judge events pertaining to parents and brothers and sisters in the Standard Horoscope.

Parents :—Pitrukaraka is Sun.

Matrukaraka is Mercury.

The 9th from Arudha Lagna is aspected by Saturn as well as by Venus, while Pitrukaraka himself is aspected by

Kuja, Kutu, Rahu and Chandra. Pitrukaraka Sun is with Atmakaraka. Pitrubhava may be said to be fairly well situated. The father died when the native was aged about 37.

The 4th from Arudha is considerably afflicted by being occupied by Kuja and Ketu and aspected by Ravi. The evil is tempered sligthtly by the aspect of Budha and Guru. Matrukaraka Budha is equally afflicted by his situation in the 8th house from Arudha and by being aspected by Kuja and Ketu. The death of the mother occurred in the Dasa of Thula (Shoola Dasa). Mark the fact of Thula as the 4th from Arudha Lagna being afflicted.

Brothers—Bhratrukaraka is Moon. The Upapada Lagna is Mesha. The third from it is occupied by malefic Saturn and the 11th by a benefic and two malefics. He had one elder brother who predeceased the native (the 11th lord himself is Saturn).

133. Marriage

In judging the affairs of marriage according to Jaimini, the starting point is the Upapada. And all the following combinations have reference to the Upapada. But we are also asked to consider the 2nd and 7th houses and their lords from Upapada as well as Darakaraka. The wife or husband will be handsome and domesticated if the 2nd house is occupied by benefics or has a predominance of benefic shadvargas or Jupiter and the Moon occupy the 7th from Karakamsa. The wife comes from a respectable or low family according as the 2nd lord is exalted or in a benefic sign or debilitated or in an inimical sign. If the 2nd house is occupied by an exalted planet the person will have many wives. The wife will be a learned woman if the 7th from Karakamsa has the association of Mercury. The person will be married to a woman in a foreign country if the Moon is in the 7th from Karakamsa. If the 2nd house happens to be a malefic sign or occupied or aspected by a malefic planet, the wife will die (early). In this particular context, the Sun should not be considered as a malefic. The wife will be older than the husband if Saturn joins the 7th from Karakamsa. The person will marry or will have liaison with a widow if Rahu is in the 7th from Karakamsa. Mars or the Sun in a similar position indicates that the marriage partner will be deformed. Wife's death will not happen if the Sun joins the 2nd house or the 2nd house happens to be Simha. Benefics aspecting the above combination lessen or neutralise the evil. More than one wife should be predicted in case the 2nd from Upapada is occupied by an exalted planet or it happens to be Gemini. If, however, the 2nd house is occupied by Atmakaraka or its own lord, then death of wife will take place late in life. The person will be obliged to reject the wife through scandals if Saturn and Rahu join the 2nd. The wife will be sickly and suffers from various types of diseases when the following combinations are present:—

Venus and Ketu in the 2nd or aspecting the 2nd from Upapada—menstrul or womb disorder; Mercury and Ketu—thinning of the bones; Saturn, Sun and Rahu—wasting disease; Saturn and Mars, the 2nd being Virgo or Gemini—Peenasa roga; Mars and Saturn, the 2nd being Aries or Scorpio—Peenasa roga; Jupiter and Saturn, the 2nd being the sign of Mars or Mercury—ear troubles; Jupiter and Rahu, the 2nd being a sign of Mars or Mercury—dental diseases; Sani and Rahu, the 2nd being Virgo or Libra—windy complaints such as dropsy. The evils in the above cases will be considerably lessened by benefic aspects. Marriage proves miserable when both Upapada and Atmakaraka signs have their second houses considerably afflicted.

Example 37

Analyse the 7th house in the Standard Horoscope.

Karaka for wife is Kuja.

The 2nd from Upapada is a benefic sign and the 2nd lord occupies a benefic (but neutral) sign. The wife came from a respectable family. The 2nd house is aspected by two first-rate malefics and the wife should have died very early had it not been for the fact that Darakaraka Mars is in a benefic sign aspected by benefics (including the Sun who is also benefic). Consequently the wife lived till the native was aged about 48. Mark the fact that the 2nd from Upapada is aspected by Mars. The wife died due to excess of bleeding at the time of an abortion.

134. Combination Applicable to Women

A woman having Jupiter in a trine from Mercury or Lagna in her Navamsa chart becomes chaste and devoted to her husband. Similar results are produced when Venus is in Lagna. Ketu in Lagna or in a trikona from Lagna (in the Navamsa) makes the lady filthy and repulsive. She will be well disposed and highly intelligent if the Moon is in Taurus in Navamsa and Mercury and Venus are in the 4th from Lagna in Navamsa. When Saturn is in Navamsa Lagna or in a trikona from it, the woman will be masculine in appearance lacking feminine grace, beauty and delicacy. She will become vindictive, filthy, uncouth and indolent if Ketu is in Navamsa Lagna or in a trikona from it. Whem Lagna is aspected by Mars, the woman becomes extremely passionate and wrathful. She will be vile, lustful and debased if Navamsa Lagna Rasi happens to be the 12th or 9th from Janma Lagna

Rasi. The Moon and Venus in Hora Lagna renders the lady amorous and sensuous. If the Navamsa of Hora Lagna is in conjunction with Ketu or aspected by malefics she becomes an adulteress. The woman would be so cruel-hearted and debased as to murder her husband if the 8th from Upapada is aspected by Mars and Ketu.

The Sun in a trikona from Lagna in the Navamsa brings about widowhood. The Moon in the 3rd from Atmakaraka or from Lagna or from Varnada Lagna definitely causes widowhood. Mars and Ketu occupying the 8th from Hora Lagna is a definite sign of early widowhood.

135. Children

The 5th house from Upapada indicates progeny while the 5th house from Lagna is also connected with issues. All combinations given in this article refer to these two factors. We are also asked to consider the 5th from the lord of Upapada in judging matters pertaining to children.

There will be a number of issues born when the 11th house from Upapada or the 5th house from Upapada lord happens to be an even sign. Predict that the person will have a number of children if the 5th from Upapada happens to be an odd sign or the Sun and Rahu are in the 7th from Upapada or its lord. Only one issue will be born when the 5th from Upapada is occupied by the Moon. The person will have no children if Mercury and Saturn join the 7th, or the Navamsa of the planet in the 7th, or the 7th lord or the Navamsa of the 7th lord. When affliction is lessened, predict issues late in life. The subject will adopt a child in case Mars and Saturn occupy the 7th or 11th from Upapada. If in the Navamsa chart, Mercury is in a trikona from Lagna, the wife becomes barren.

Example 38

Judge details pertaining to children in the Standard Horoscope.

The 5th from Upapada is an odd sign. The 5th lord from Upapada is in the 11th from Upapada and is fairly strong. The subject had a number of issues.

136. Profession

In Parasari, the 10th house rules occupation, fame and honour. But in Jaimini, Karakamsa seems to play important part in indicating the nature of profession one is likely to pursue. Though the particular nature of the occupation is difficult to judge, yet by a careful study and investigation of the methods formulated by Jaimini, it may be possible to discover principles which could give a definite clue in the matter of choice of profession. The following combinations are to be applied with reference to Karakamsa. If the Karakamsa or its 10th is not occupied by any planet, take the lord of the 10th from Karakamsa and judge profession considering his position in the Navamsa.

The Sum in Karakamsa confers political leadership or State service. Full Moon and Venus in Karakamsa give rise to authors, preceptors and to those who make a living by the dissemination of knowledge. When Mars is in the amsa of Atmakaraka then a profession involving dealing with factories, printing presses, chemicals, fires and metallurgy will be involved. Mercury makes one a businessman, sculptor, artist, cloth merchant and well-versed in classical lore. Jupiter in Karakamsa produces a deep scholar in religious subjects and a profound philosopher. Venus in Karakamsa gives rise to authors, rulers, ministers and Government officers. Saturn makes one a well-known businessman. When Rahu is in Karakamsa, the person ekes out livelihood by Dhanurvidya or as a druggist, swindler or a profession involving manufacture of machinery; or one may become a mechanic. Ketu renders the person earn his livelihood by fraudulent and deceitful means. Rahu and Ravi in Karakamsa devoid of afflictions indicate doctors solely dealing with poisonous drugs, or preferably chemists and druggists; one lives by the art of swindling others if Karakamsa Rasi falls in the sign of Gulika (see art. 34) and aspected by Moon. The person lives by the performance of sacrifices and other religious ceremonies when Karakamsa joined by Ketu is aspected by Venus. The Sun and Venus aspecting Karakamsa makes one an ambassador or servant of the Crown. The Sun in the 10th aspected by Jupiter alone—the person lives by protecting cattle, *i.e.*, by running a dairy farm or the like. Malefics in the 3rd and 6th from Karakamsa give rise to agriculture and gardening, Guru in the 9th from Karakamsa denotes income through large estates or landed properties.. One may take to alchemy if the Moon occupying Karakamsa is aspected by Venus. The person will be a doctor if the Karakamsa occupied by Moon is aspected by Mercury. If Saturn occupies Karakamsa or the 4th from it, the person becomes skilled in using arms and consequently may take to police or military career. One becomes a watch-maker or horologist if Karakamsa or the 4th from it is joined by Ketu. Rahu in the position suggested above may give a profession like manufacturing machinery or mining. The Sun or Mars in the 4th from Karakamsa makes the person live by bearing different kinds of arms. The Moon and Jupiter in the Karakamsa or in the 5th from it indicates that the person becomes a famous writer, author, editor or a journalist. If instead of Jupiter, Venus joins the above position, the person will be a mediocre writer, author or editor. One becomes a great poet or literateur if Sukra alone joins Karakamsa or the 5th from it. Guru in the above position confers all-round knowledge and the person becomes an author. A person becomes a high official of the Government if Guru or Sukra occupies the 5th from the lords of Lagna and the 7th. If malefics from lords of Lagna and the 7th are posited in the 3rd or 6th, one becomes a Commander. When the malefic and benefic influences in respect of Karakamsa are evenly disposed, the subject becomes a leader of his community.

It will be seen from the above that the position of Karakamsa and the disposition of planets in certain houses from it are the main considerations in determining the avocation or nature of livelihood. The strength of the combinations will be augmented or weakened according as the planets and signs concerned are under benefic or malefic argalas. A careful study of the sutras suggests that the following allocation of professions could be made to the different planets.

The Sun :—Presidents, Kings, Ministers and other high ranking Government services.

The Moon :— Ministers and high officers of the Government.

Mars :— Commanders-in-chief, scientists and fire industries.

Mercury : Professors of philosophy, authors, artists, sculptors, weavers, journalists, editors, lawyers, intellectuals and even businessmen.

Jupiter :—Priests, judges, professors of philosophy and leaders in general.

Venus : Officials of the Government, ambassadors and representatives of ruling heads.

Saturn: Ordinary or common professions, manufacture of arms and ammunitions, hardware merchants, printing, body-guards, etc.

Rahu :—Thieves, body-guards, doctors and healers.

Ketu :- Servants, labourers, drivers, mechanics. masons and brick-layers.

Example 39

Judge the profession in the Standard Horoscope.

Neither the Karakamsa nor the 10th from Karakamsa have any planets in them. The 10th lord from Karakamsa is associated with the Sun, Venus and Mars, while the 10th is aspected by Rahu and Ketu. Consequently, the strong position of the 10th lord from Karakamsa and his association with the planets mentioned above should decide the profession, *viz.*, Saturn—businessman : Mars—dealing with printing presses, etc ; Venus—author. Thus different professions are indicated.

137. Source of Death

We have already discussed in articles 101 to 123 the methods of ascertaining longevity and death-inflicting Rasis. In the course of this article, I shall record the circumstances under which death actually takes place, *i.e.*, whether the end will be natural, violent, or peaceful and the character of the violent, natural or peaceful death. I have merely given the principles culled out from Jaimini and it is for readers to convince themselves about their practical applicability or otherwise.

138. Nature of Death

According to commentators of Jaimini, *Dushta Marana*, or violent end means death caused by fires, explosions, earthquakes, drownings, volcanic eruptions, falls from eminences, etc. Subha Marana or natural death means the end being brought about by fevers and other diseases. When malefics are in the 3rd from Lagna or Atmakaraka, the person will have an unnatural death. Benefics denote natural death. Here also good aspects interposing among afflictions and bad aspects interposing among benefic dispositions will often change the nature of death. In considering the following combinations, whenever a conjunction is meant, aspect is also automatically implied.

When the 3rd house from Lagna or from Atmakaraka is conjoined with (or aspected by) the Sun, death will be due to political offences, *viz.*, hanging, beheading, etc.; Mars—fire, weapons and injuries; Saturn and Gulika—poisons, snake-bites, incarcerations and drownings; and Moon and Gulika—by eating hard and indigestible food. Death can happen by snake-bite if Rahu and Ravi are in Karakamsa.

When the 3rd house from Lagna or from Atmakaraka is occupied (or aspected) by the Moon, death will be due to consumption; Saturn—windy diseases, rheumatism; Ketu—dropsy and other watery diseases; Jupiter—indigestion, vomitings and inflammation of the phlegm; Venus—sexual and female diseases such as syphillis and gonorrhoea. When a number of planets are connected with the 3rd house, death will be caused by various complications and miscellaneous diseases.

When the house of death, *i.e.*, the 3rd from Lagna or Atmakaraka is occupied by benefics, death takes place in holy places, or near temples, churches and mosques. If malefics are in the 3rd death takes place in evil surroundings, *i.e.*, in places where sins are committed. The native will be conscious or unconscious at the time of death according as the 3rd is occupied (or aspected) by Jupiter and Venus, or other planets.

Example 40

Find the nature and sources of death in the Standard Horoscope.

The third is Cancer, a benefic sign and it is not occupied by any malefics. The person should have a natural death. The third is aspected by three planets—Sun, Mercury and Jupiter—the strongest being Jupiter. The end was due to some sort of inflammation of the phlegm and he was conscious when he breathed his last.

139. Yogas in Jaimini

For purposes of convenience, I propose to deal with Yogas as per Jaimini system under three distinct categories, *viz.*, Raja Yogas, Arishta Yogas, and Miscellaneous Yogas which include Sanyasa Yogas, Vahana Yogas, etc.

140. Raja Yogas

When Janma Lagna, Hora Lagna and Ghatika Lagna are aspected by a planet, a powerful Raja Yoga is caused and the person becomes a king or an equal to him. If one or two of the Lagnas are aspected, then the Yoga is not formed It is not clear whether all the three Lagnas should be aspected by the same planet or by different planets.

A Raja Yoga is said to arise if in Rasi, Navamsa and Drekkana the Lagna and the 7th are conjoined with or aspected by a planet. The person becomes a king. The intensity of the Yoga is reduced if aspect or association of a planet is not found in all the six factors. If the same planet aspects, the Yoga becomes *par excellence.*

Raja Yoga can also arise if either in (*a*) Navamsa or in (*b*) Drekkana diagrams, the Lagna, Hora Lagna and Ghatika Lagna are aspected by (or associated with) a planet. In all the above cases, the condition for the existence of an all-powerful Raja Yoga is that all the three factors and not merely one or two should have the relationship of a planet. By implication—and the commentators seem to confirm this, it means that if only one factor (Lagna or Hora Lagna or Ghatika Lagna) is involved, the yoga can operate nominally or formally. Some commentators hold that the three factors (Lagna, Hora Lagna and Ghatika Lagna) should be aspected by the same planet.

When Mars, Venus and Ketu are in mutual aspects or in the 3rd from each other, an ordinary type of Raja Yoga known as Vaithanica will arise, conferring on the native distinction and fame.

Raja Yogas are formed under the following conditions :

(1) When the 2nd, 4th and 5th from Atmakaraka are equal in strength or are occupied by benefics, (2) when the 3rd and 6th from Atmakaraka are of equal strength or are occupied by malefics and (3) when the 2nd, 4th and 5th from the lord of Lagna or from the lord of the 7th are occupied or aspected by benefics. When the influences are mixed, one becomes an equal to a ruler but not an actual ruler.

The position of Venus in Karakamsa in highly favoured as it is said to confer immense fortune and life.

The following are also Raja Yogas capable of conferring different grades of political power, fame, and rank consistent with their vitality.

(*a*) Lords of Lagna and the 5th in conjunction, and exalted or debilitated or in their own Navamsas—a great ruler.

(*b*) When the Yoga is merely due to an association between lord of Lagna and the 5th, or 7th and 5th, it makes itself expressed rather late in life.

(*c*) Venus, Mars and Ketu in Atmakaraka Rasi and 2nd and 4th respectively from it—a king.

(*d*) The strong disposition of Lagna, the 7th and 9th —political power.

(*e*) Same number of planets in Lagna and the 7th : Raja Yoga forms but it will be enjoyed by the native late in life.

(*f*) Equal number of planets in Lagna and 4th—fame and honour.

(*g*) Jupiter and Moon in Lagna and the 11th respectively or in Lagna and the 7th aspected by benefics—Ruler.

(*h*) Raja Yoga in early life if Mercury and Jupiter in Lagna and 11th or Lagna and 7th aspected by benefics.

(*i*) Venus and Moon in conjunction with or aspecting Atmakaraka or the 10th from him.

(*j*) Moon in the 7th in conjunction with or aspected by benefics—a servant of the Crown.

(*k*) Thrikonas and Kendras devoid of benefics—servant of king.

(*l*) Benefics or planets with benefic vargas occupying Atmakaraka Rasi or the 10th from it—moderate Raja Yoga.

(*m*) The Moon in the 4th or 11th from Jupiter in Navamsa—Fame and power.

(*n*) Benefics in Janma Rasi and in the 11th and 10th in Navamsa—fairly powerful Raja Yoga.

(*o*) The Lagna and Atmakaraka Rasi being occupied or aspected by exalted planet—a ruler.

(*p*) The Navamsa Rasi of Atmakaraka same as Lagna or Janma Rasi or the Rasi occupied by Jupiter—Raja Yoga of a fairly high order.

(*q*) Same number of benefics in Arudha Lagna and the Navamsa Rasi of the 9th—political power.

(*r*) Malefics in the 3rd and 6th from Atmakaraka or Arudha Lagna—Ruler.

We are asked by Jaimini to study Raja Yogas, when the starting point is not definitely mentioned, from Lagna, Atmakaraka and the 5th.

Raja Yogas given by Jaimini have not been tested as his method has not been in vogue. It is for readers to try, apply the various Yogas to practical example and then see how far they could be made use of for predicting power and fame.

Example 41

Describe Raja Yogas, if any, in the Standard Horoscope.

The following Raja Yogas are present :—

(*a*) Janma Lagna is aspected by Kuja and Ketu. Hora Lagna and Ghatika Lagna are aspected by the same planets, *viz.*, Jupiter, the Sun and Mercury—hence a fairly powerful Raja Yoga.

(*b*) The Navamsa Lagna, Hora Lagna and Ghatika Lagna are occupied by Jupiter, Rahu and Ketu respectively—fairly powerful Raja Yoga.

(*c*) Excepting the 10th Kendra, all the other Kendras and Thrikonas are devoid of occupation by benefics.

(*d*) Karakamsa is the same sign as the Janma Rasi.

It might interest readers to learn that the native enjoyed all the blessings of Raja Yoga, short of wielding power.

141. Arishta Yogas

These refer only to dire misfortunes. But I have included in this section combinations that make one diabolical or criminal in his temper. The following combinations should be of special interest.

Ketu in Karakamsa—thief ; the Sun and Rahu in Karakamsa aspected by Mars—delights in setting fire to others' houses ; Ketu in the Karakamsa aspected by Budha and Sani—becomes a eunuch. The shadvargas of Sukra and Kuja predominating in the 9th from Karakamsa—seeks sexual gratification through women other than his own wife. The person will be hen-pecked if the 9th from Karakamsa is aspected by or associated with Guru. Malefics in the 2nd and 8th from Janma Lagna or Janma Arudha—misfortunes and poverty. Mercury in the 12th from Lagnarudha—loss of money through litigation. Same number of planets in the 2nd and 12th or 5th and 9th or 12th and 6th or 10th and 4th—imprisonment. Same number of planets in the 2nd and 9th—great misfortunes. Rahu in the Arudha of the 5th house aspected by the Sun—loss of sight. Karakamsa having the shadvargas of Saturn or Karakamsa being associated with Sani, Rahu or other malefics—the native will be an illegitimate issue. Gulika in Karakamsa makes one to administer poison to others. Or he will himself die by poison being administered to him.

142. Miscellaneous Yogas

Some of the combinations grouped here will be found to be useful in gratifying the curiosities of the limited few who may be interested in things other than purely mundane.

A person gets vehicles and horses if the Moon and Venus are in mutual aspects or the Moon is in the 3rd from Venus or both are in the 2nd. If the Moon and Venus aspect the 4th from Karakamsa one acquires fine and beautiful houses. Rahu and Sani in the 4th from Karakamsa give houses built in stone while Kuja and Ketu enable one to acquire houses built in brick. When the Sun is in the 4th, he lives in thatched huts and improvised structures.

Malefics in the 2nd from Upapada reveal that one becomes an ascetic. If the Moon and the 7th are in conjunction with benefics, one becomes a mahant or a religious head.

If the Atmakaraka occupies the Navamsa of Kumbha, the person builds tanks and choultries and lays parks for public benefit. He will also be inclined to do charitable deeds if the Karakamsa happens to be Meena. One will have Moksha or final emancipation if benefics occupy the 12th from Karakamsa, or if Karakamsa being Aries or Sagittarius is occupied by Ketu. One will have devotion for Siva, Gouri, Lakshmi, Shanmukha, Vishnu, Sambasiva, Durga and Ganapathi, provided Karakamsa has the association of Ravi, Chandra, Sukra, Kuja, Budha, Guru and Ketu respectively. The person will worship Kshudra devathas or lower forms of deities if Karakamsa being an immovable sign and joined by Saturn or Venus. Similar results accrue if Amatyakaraka is in Karakamsa. One becomes a mantravadi if both the 5th and 9th from Karakamsa have one malefic each. Faith in God should be judged from the Devatakaraka. If the Devatakaraka is a benefic he will worship a benevolent deity ; if a malefic a cruel deity. The devotion will be sincere or otherwise according as the Devatakaraka is exalted and otherwise strong or debilitated or otherwise weak.

CHAPTER VIII

Timing Events

143. General Remarks

Timing or calculation of future events has always been a hard nut to crack. The birth horoscope is significant for the whole life and according to Parasara, the results due to various combinations come into operation during the various Dasas and Bhuktis influenced to some extent by the Gochara or transits of planets. Here in Jaimini, we have a unique method of approach to the whole problem of direction. There is no mention of either planetary Dasas or Gochara, though nevertheless there are suggestions in works like *Jathaka Rajeeya* and *Vanchanatheeya* which are mainly based upon Jaimini that Rasi Dasa influences are affected by transits. There are quite a number of Dasas in Jaimini and these have been referred to in article 73. What are the specific conditions under which the different Dasa systems should be applied to different events? No clear instructions have been given in this matter by the commentators, even though here and there a hint is thrown, upon which one has to draw one's own inferences. Pandits, with whom I had the pleasure of discussing this matter, are of divided opinion. Some say that Chara Dasa is the Sage's favourite system for predicting all important events, basing their authority on Adhyaya 1, Pada 2, Sutra 121, in which Jaimini says that "all combinations mentioned earlier fructify during or in the beginning of the various Rasi Dasas". I am unable to offer any concrete help in this regard for the number of horoscopes to which I have applied the various Dasas of Jaimini are not adequate enough to warrant any categorical opinions or statements. I would rather rely upon the opinions of scholars until forced to revise my views by what I would call "experimental evidence". Sthira Dasa is supposed to be equally reliable not only in ascertaining death but also in predicting other events while Thrikona Dasa in the cases worked out by our Research Section have yielded encouraging results. Niryana Shula Dasa appears to be quite useful in predicting death of parents, brothers, sisters and relatives, while Niryana Phala Shula Desa, mainly intended for predicting one's own demise and probably applicable to only Madhyayus-horoscopes, could be considered to be purely of academic interest. It occurs to me that all the various methods of Dasa reckoning grew side by side and were attempts to develop correct methods of timing events, probably by a process of hit and miss. As my task is not to advocate but to simply render a faithful account of Jaimini's principles, as I have understood them, I leave it to my intelligent readers to decide for themselves the choice of a Dasa. I can only add that the consensus of opinion is in favour of both Chara and Sthira Dasas for predicting important events, and Niryana Shula Dasa for ascertaining the periods of death of one's parents, brothers, sisters, wife and relatives.

144. Nature of Results

As in Parasari, several considerations have to be taken note of in judging the results of Dasas and Bhuktis. As a general proposition, it may be stated that a Rasi during its Dasa generally gives the results pertaining to the house it refers to from Karakamsa or from Arudha Lagna. Rasis occupied by exalted planets, or their own lords, generally confer favourable results in their Dasas. Apart from the relation a particular Rasi whose Dasa is under consideration bears to Karakamsa, Atmakaraka, etc., the capacity of a Rasi for producing benefic or mischievous results seem to depend to a large extent upon certain harmonious or inharmonious dispositions of planets from the Rasi concerned. Thus malefics in the 2nd give financial losses. When the 5th Rasi is occupied by the Sun or the Moon in association with Saturn, or the Moon and Rahu are in the 6th and 8th, the subject comes under the wrath of the Government. On the other hand, the Sun's disposition in the 6th gives favours from superiors and access to wealth. When malefics are on either side of the Rasi, or in the 8th, or in the Rasi concerned, there will be troubles, misfortunes, losses and a generally unfavourable period during the Rasi Dasa. The positions of Guru in a Kendra is recommended. In the above combinations and the following ones, I am supported by works such as *Vanchanateeya,* which have been primarily based on Jaimini. The following rules of Dasa interpretation, culled from the same sources, may be taken note of: (*a*) A Rasi Dasa confers wealth if the Moon and Venus are in the 3rd, (*b*) loss of wealth if these planets are in the 12th, (*c*) Rahu in the 12th—fever and other bodily ailments, (*d*) Rahu in the Rasi, foreign travels, (*e*) malefics in the 9th—danger to father. Taking the Dasa Rasi as corresponding to Lagna and considering the benefic or malefic influences centered on the appropriate Rasis therefrom, fortunate or unfortunate results may be anticipated. Thus if malefics are in the 4th, we have to infer mother's health will be in danger.

Of the Dasas of the various Rasis, those of Thula, Kataka, Vrishabha, Mesha, Dhanus, Kanya and Mithuna are said to generally give rise to favourable results, the good decreasing gradually from Thula to Mithuna in the order given above. Simha, Mesha, Kumbha, Vrischika and Makara generally confer evil results, the degree of evil increasing gradually in the order given above. In short, the nature of the results of a Rasi Dasa should be measured by a consideration of the strength or weakness of the lord and the afflictions the lord and the Rasi are subjected to.

Upon the hint given by Jaimini in the last sutra of Adhyaya 1, Pada 2, to which reference is made in article 143 we may formulate a general principle that the results pertaining to a certain combination will come into fruition in the Dasa and Bhukti of the Rasis involved in the formation of the concerned combination. Take for instance, Adhyaya I, P. 1, S. 42. The Moon and Venus in the 4th from Karakamsa give palatial buildings. Suppose Karakamsa is Mesha. Then the combination has reference to Karkataka or the 4th. The Dasa of Karkataka can enable the person to acquire houses and other properties provided, it has no afflictions such as those already indicated above.

145. Father's Death

(*i*) The stronger one between the Sun and Venus should be considered as Pitrumaraka. If the weaker planet between the Sun and Venus happens to be aspected by a malefic, then that becomes the Pitrumaraka. Death of the father takes place in the Dasa of the Shula Rasis

The basis for ascertaining the strengths of Rasis for purposes of applying Niryana Shula Dasas is, according to some, the Rasi being occupied by planets and the longitudes of the lord of the particular Rasis.

(1st, 5th and 9th), (*a*) from Pitrumaraka Rasi, *i.e.*, the sign occupied by the lord of the 8th from Pitrumaraka. Suppose for instance Pitrumaraka is Venus and his longitude is 20° Virgo, and the lord of the 8th from Pitrumaraka is Mars, his longitude being 24° Taurus. Then Mars is stronger. Death of the father will happen in the Dasa of the 1st, 5th or 9th Rasi from Taurus (the Rasi held by Mars). (*ii*) Take the 9th from Lagna and the 9th from 7th. See which is more powerful. Death of the father will take place in the Niryana Shula Dasa (see art. 98) of the more powerful Rasi. For example suppose that Aquarius and Simha are the 9th from Lagna and from 7th respectively and that Simha is the stronger Rasi. Then death of father can be predicted in the Shula Dasas of Simha (1st), Dhanus (5th) or Mesha (9th). Between the two methods given above, the latter is supposed to be more reliable, as it is specially intended for predicting death events.

Example 42

Find the maraka period of the father in the Standard Horoscope.

(*i*) Pitrumarakas are the Sun and Venus.

∵ Venus has greater longitude, he is stronger than the Sun.

He could become Pitrumaraka.

The Sun is aspected by a malefic.

∴ The Sun could become Pitrumaraka.

But since Venus is also aspected by a malefic Saturn, the stronger of the two, *viz.*, Venus is Pitrumaraka. The 8th lord from Venus is the Moon. Between Venus and the Moon, Venus is stronger because of greater longitude. Death of father can take place in the Dasa of Dhanus (1st), Mesha (5th) and Simha (9th).

By the end of Simha Dasa (see page 78 & 79) the native was aged 36 years. The father actually died in the 37th year of the native.

(*ii*) The 9th from Lagna and the 9th from 7th are, respectively, Capricorn and Cancer. The latter is the stronger (see Ex. 18).

∴ Father's death can, take place in Karkataka, Vrischika or Meena. Meena is ruled out as the Dasa comes very late in life. Between Vrischika and Karkataka the latter is stronger as its lord has greater longitude. The Shula Dasa of Karkataka lasts for 9 years from 36 to 45 Father died as soon as Karkataka Dasa commenced.

146. Mother's Death

(*i*) The stronger between Mars and the Moon becomes Matrumaraka. If the weaker between these two is aspected by a malefic, that becomes Matrumaraka (*a*). Death of the mother takes in the (Chara) Dasa of Shula Rasis (1, 5 and 9) from (*a*), the 8th from Matrumaraka Rasi or (*b*) from the Rasi held by the lord of the 8th from Matrumaraka Rasi.

(*ii*) Ascertain the stronger Rasi between the 4th from Lagna and the 4th from the 7th. Death of the mother may be predicted in the Niryana Shula Dasa of the 1st, 5th or 9th from the stronger Rasi.

Example 43

Find the period of mother's death in the Standard Horoscope.

(*i*) Moon and Mars are Matrumarakas. Moon (18° 29') is stronger than Mars (0° 53'). Mars as well as the Moon are aspected by the malefic Sun. Hence, the stronger planet, the Moon, alone is Matrumaraka.

The 8th lord from Matrumaraka is Mars.

Hence prefer the Moon.

∴ Mother's death can take place in Shula Rasis of Mesha, *viz.*, Mesha, Simha and Dhanus. Of the three, Mesha is the strongest as it has two planets.

Mesha Dasa lasted (see page 54 & 55) till the age of 13, within which period mother died.

(*ii*) The 4th Rasis from Lagna and from 7th are Simha and Kumbha respectively. Kumbha is stronger than Simha, as the former has planets in it. Therefore mother's death can take place in the Shula Dasa of Kumbha, Mithuna or Thula. Kumbha is ruled out as it comes when the native is aged nearly 80 years. Between Thula and Mithuna, Thula is the stronger, as it has two planets. Shula Dasa of Thula lasts from 9 to 15 years during which period the native lost his mother. Actually the sub-period was that of Mithuna.

147. Native's Own Death

Elsewhere, rules for the determination of Maraka Rasis have been given in detail. In this article, I merely propose to refer to the method of predicting the native's own death according to Shula Dasa. Find the stronger of the Lagna and the 7th. Death happens in Shula Dasa of the stronger Rasi or the 5th or 9th from it.

Example 44

Find the period of native's death according to article 147.

Between Lagna and the 7th, Lagna alone is stronger (see Ex. 18.). Therefore death can happen in the Shula Dasa of Vrishabha, Kanya or Makara. Since the horoscope belongs to the category of Purnayu, Makara is the death-inflicting Rais. The Shula Dasa of Makara runs from 90 to 99 years. The subject did just when he completed 81 years.

148. Death of Wife

(*i*) This can happen in the (Chara) Dasas of the Rasi held by Jupiter and the 5th and 9th from it. In judging the probable period of death, due consideration should be given to the general strength of the Bhava in question.

Example 45

Find the period of death of the wife in the Standard Horoscope.

Jupiter is in Kumbha. Death may happen in the Dasa of Kumbha, Mithuna and Thula. Kumbha Dasa terminates when the native would be aged 24. The 7th house is fairly strong. Therefore wife's death is possible in the Dasa of Thula, the stronger between Thula and Mithuna. Thula Dasa extends till the native completes his 46th year. Death happened just at the end of 46th year.

149. Death of Other Relatives

(*i*) Taking into consideration the positions of Putra and Matula and other Karakas, death of the respective relatives may be predicted in the (Chara) Dasa of the respective Shula Rasis.

(ii) Take the stronger Rasi between the 3rd from Lagna and 3rd from the 7th, and predict the death of brothers in the appropriate Niryana Shula Dasa. Death of children can happen in the Niryana Shula Dasa of 1st, 5th and 9th Rasis from the stronger Rasi between the Rasis from Lagna and the 5th from 7th.

The elder brother's death can be anticipated in the

Shula Dasas of the 1st, 5th and 9th Rasis from the stronger Rasi between the 11th from Lagna and the 7th.

In predicting all these events, the indications must be first ascertained by carefully studying the birth horoscope. If for instance, a birth chart does not show indications for the birth of children, then the question of timing the event of the death of children does not arise at all.

Example 46

Find the probable periods of death of brothers and children in the Standard Horoscope.

Younger Brothers

The 3rd Rasis from Lagna and 7th are respectively Cancer and Makara. Cancer is the stronger. Death of younger brothers (if any) can happen in the Shula Dasa of Cancer, Scorpio and Pisces.

Elder Brothers

The 11th Rasis from Lagna and 7th respectively are Meena and Kanya. Meena is the stronger. Therefore elder brother's death can happen in the Shula Dasa of Meena, Kataka or Vrischika.

Children

The 5th Rasis from Lagna and the 7th are respectively Kanya and Meena. The latter is the stronger. Therefore death of children can happen in the Shula Dasa of Meena Kataka or Vrischika.

CHAPTER IX

Summary

150. General Observations

Though Jaimini and Parasari systems of Astrology appear to be different, actually Jaimini is merely an offshoot of Parasari, developed according to the genius of the Sage and presented in the shape of sutras or aphorisms not capable of easy comprehension or understanding unless aided by commentaries. Jaimini's speciality consists in the importance given to Karakamsa and Arudha Lagna, in the simplicity of methods used for the determination of plnnetary strengths and longevity, and the original and unique approach to the problem of directions or Dasas. The selection of an appropriate Dasa for predicting an appropriate event has been a matter of controversy. The intelligent reader should try to discover for himself the type of Dasa that suits a particular horoscope or a particular event or set of events. There is no doubt that pride of place has been given to Chara Dasa.

151. Karakas

According to Jaimini, Karakas vary with regard to each horoscope. There are seven main Karakas, *viz.*, Atma, Amatya, Bhratru, Matru, Putra, Gnathi and Dara. Convert the longitudes of planets into signs, degrees, etc. Reject the signs and considering the degrees, etc., tabulate the positions of planets in the descending order of the number of degrees. The planet that gets the highest degree becomes Atmakaraka. In the order of Karakas given above, the other planets become Amatya, Bhratru, etc., according to the descending order of degrees. When two or more planets hold the same longitude, there will be a merging of Karakas and those falling vacant will have to be filled up by Rahu and the appropriate natural Karakas.

Example 47

Find the various Karakas in the horoscope of Herr Hitler, born on 24–4–1889 at 6-30 p.m. (L.M.T.) corresponding to Gh. 33-30 after sunrise, Lat. 48° N., Long. 13° E.

Planetary positions in the horoscope are :—

Planet	*Rasi*	*Degree*	*Minute*
The Sun	Mesha	9	56
The Moon	Dhanus	15	46
Mars	Mesha	25	31
Mercury	Mesha	4	48
Jupiter	Dhanus	17	23
Venus	Mesha	25	50
Saturn	Kataka	22	35
Rahu	Mithuna	25	6
Ketu	Dhanus	25	6
Lagna	Thula	4	54

The following are the Rasi and Navamsa diagrams :—

	Sun Mars Mer. Venus	Hora Lagna	Rahu
	RASI		Saturn Varnada & Ghatika Lagnas
Moon Jupit. Ketu		Lagna Arudha Lagna	

		Mer. Rahu	Sun
	NAVAMSA		
Sat.			Moon
	Karakamsa Mars Venus Lagna Ketu		Jupit.

Tabulating the positions of planets according to the descending order of their degrees, etc., we have :—

Planet	*Rasi*	*Degree*	*Minute*
Sukra	Mesha	25	50
Kuja	Mesha	25	31
Sani	Kataka	22	35
Guru	Dhanus	17	23
Chandra	Dhanun	15	46
Ravi	Mesha	9	56
Budha	Mesha	4	48

Since Sukra has the highest longitude, he becomes the *Atmakaraka*. The other Karakas are as follows :—

Karaka	*Lord*
Atmakaraka	Sukra
Amatyakaraka	Kuja
Bhratrukaraka	Sani
Matrukaraka	Guru
Putrakaraka	Chandra
Gnatikaraka	Ravi
Darakaraka	Budha

152. Different Kinds of Lagnas

Of the various Lagnas referred to by Jaimini, Arudha Lagna, Hora Lagna, Varnada and Ghatika Lagna are important in the judgment of a horoscope, especially in regard to the application of Raja Yogas. Arudha Lagna is the sign arrived at by counting as many signs from Lagna as lord of Lagna is from Lagna. Hora Lagna is represented by the sign arrived at by counting the quotient (obtained by dividing birth time in ghatis from sunrise by 2·5) plus *one* from the Sun or Lagna according as the Lagna is odd or even. The process involved in finding Varnada Lagna is this : According as Janma Lagna is odd or even count clockwise or anti-clockwise from Mesha or Meena to Lagna. Call this 'a'. Deal with Hora Lagna similarly and obtain 'b'. Then the sum of, or difference between, 'a' and 'b' represents 'c' according as both Janma and Hora Lagnas are odd, or one is odd and the other is even. Varnada is the Rasi arrived at by counting 'c' from Mesha (direct) or Meena (reverse) according as Lagna is odd or even. Ghatika Lagna can be obtained by adding to the 1st degree of Lagna Rasi the product of time of birth (in ghatis) × 30.

Example 48

Find out Arudha, Hora, Varnada, Bhava and Ghatika Lagnas in Hitler's horoscope.

Arudha Lagna :—The lord of Lagna Sukra is in the 7th, and the 7th from the 7th, *viz*., Lagna itself will be Arudha Lagna.

∴ Arudha Lagna = Thula.

Hora Lagna :– Dividing the birth ghatis by 2·5, we (33·5/2·5) = 13 as quotient and ·1 as remainder. Expunging 12 and counting 2 $(n+1)$ from the

Sun, as Janma Lagna is odd, we get Vrishabha as Hora Lagna. The remainder, *viz.*, ·1 multiplied by 30 gives 12°.

∴ Hora Lagna = Vrishabha 12°.

Bhava Lagna :—Janma Lagna is Thula, an odd sign. Birth Ghatis = 33·5.

$$\therefore n = \frac{33\cdot 5}{5} - 6\cdot 7 = \text{Quotient 6 and Remainder } 0\cdot 7.$$

∵ Janma Lagna is odd, Bhava Lagna is the 7th (6 + 1) from the Sun, *viz.*, Thula : Converting the remainder we get 21°.

∴ Bhava Lagna = Thula 21·

Varnada Lagna :—Janma Lagna is Thula, an odd sign. Hora Lagna is Vrishabha, an even sign.

∵ $a = 7$ (counting direct from Mesha to Janma Lagna).

$b = 11$ (counting backwards from Meena to Hora Lagna).

∵ Janma Lagna is odd and Hora Lagna is even, take the difference between a and b, which is equal to 4. As Janma Lagna is an odd sign counting 4 from Mesha we get Kataka.

∴ Varnada Lagna = Kataka.

Ghatika Lagna :—Janma Lagna is Thula.

Birth Time in Ghatis = 33·5.

Dividing the birth ghatis by 12,

we get $\frac{33\cdot 5}{12}$ 9·5 as remainder

The integral part is 9 (n) and factional part. 5. Ghatika Lagna is the Rasi arrived at by counting $n+1$ $(9+1)$ from Janma Lagna.

∴ Ghatika Lagna – Kataka 15°.

Pranapada is a certain sensitive point which can be obtained by adding twice the birth time (in vighatis) to (*a*) the Sun's longitude, (*b*) the Sun's longitude + 240° or (*c*) the Sun's longitude + 120° according as the Sun is in a movable, fixed or common sign.

Dwara Rasi is the sign whose Dasa is under consideration either for judging certain events of life or the maraka period.

Bahya Rasi is the sign which is as many signs away from Dwara, as Dwara is from Lagna.

Gulika, to whom importance is given by Jaimini, is said to preside over the part of time (obtained by dividing the duration of a day or duration of night by 8) allotted to Saturn.

Brahma, Maheswara and Rudra are all certain distinctions conferred on planets by virtue of certain horoscopic dispositions. Brahma's position is important for calculating Sthira and Brahma Dasas and Rudra and Maheswara are considered to ascertain the death-inflicting Rasi.

Example 49

Find Gulika, Brahma, Maheswara and Rudra in Hitler's horoscope.

Gulika (Art 34) :—Weekday of birth : Saturday. Duration of day, *viz.*, Gh. 34·4 divided by 8 gives 4·3.

∴ Saturn's part extends from sunrise to 4·3 ghatis.

∴ Gulika's position corresponds to the rising degree at Ghs. 4·3 from sunrise. = *Vrishabha 17° 57'*.

Brahma (Art. 35) :—Between Lagna and the 7th, the latter is stronger = A (*vide* Art. 53). Lords of 6, 8 and 12 from A are Mercury, Mars and Jupiter respectively. Among these three, Mars is the strongest. Next comes Jupiter (*vide* Art. 59). But Mars not being in the visible half (from the 7th) Jupiter should be considered as the Brahma as he is not only in the visible half but in an odd sign also.

∴ Brahma is Jupiter.

Maheswara (Art. 38) :—The lord of the 8th from Atmakaraka is Mars. He is in his own house. 12th lord is Jupiter. So we have to choose the stronger of the 8th and 12th lords from Atmakaraka, *viz.*, Mars and Jupiter. The former is stronger. Hence Maheswara is Mars.

Rudra (Art. 39) :—The lords of the 2nd and 8th from Lagna are Mars and Venus respectively. Because Venus is stronger than Mars, he is Rudra.

153. Aspects and Argalas

All movable signs aspect all fixed signs except the adjacent ones. All fixed signs aspect all movable signs except the adjacent ones. All common signs aspect each other. Argalas may be defined as 'agents' promoting or obsructing flow of fortunate vibrations in a horoscope. Planets in the 4th, 2nd, 11th or 5th from an aspecting body cause Argalas. These are countered by a simultaneous disposition of planets in the 10th, 12th, 3rd or 9th. A number of malefics in the 3rd can also give rise to Papargala. Ketu is an exception. Planets in the 9th from Ketu cause Argala which gets neutralised when there are planets in the 5th. For the benefic or malefic nature of Argalas, refer to articles 45 and 46.

Example 50

Find out the Argalas in Hitler's horoscope and prepare an Argala Chart.

Planetary Argalas in Hitler's Horoscope

Planet	*Argala caused by*	*Counteracted by*
Ravi	Sani	None
Chandra	Ravi, Budha, Sukra, Kuja	,,
Kuja	Sani	,,
Budha	Sani	,,
Guru	Ravi, Budha, Sukra, Kuja	,,
Sukra	Sani	,,
Sani	None	,,
Rahu	Sani, Ravi, Budha, Sukra, Kuja	,,
Ketu	None	,,

<table>
<tr><td>Sani
Ravi
Kuja
Sukra
Budha
Rahu (Chandra, Guru, Ketu)</td><td>Sani</td><td>Rahu (Ravi, Kuja, Sukra, Budha)</td><td>Sani
Ravi
Kuja
Sukra
Budha</td></tr>
<tr><td>Rahu
Chandra
Guru
Ketu
(Ravi, Budha, Kuja, Sukra)</td><td colspan="2" rowspan="2">ARGALA CHAKRA</td><td></td></tr>
<tr><td>Kuja
Ravi
Sukra
Budha</td><td>Rahu
Guru
Chandra
Ketu
(Ravi, Kuja, Budha, Sukra)</td></tr>
<tr><td>Kuja
Ravi
Sukra
Budha</td><td>Guru
Chandra
Ketu</td><td></td><td>Guru
Chandra
Ketu
Sani
(Rahu)</td></tr>
</table>

In the above chart, Sani has been placed in Mesha to denote the Argala caused by him to Mesha Rasi as well as planets situated therein. It should also be noted that there is no opposition to his Argala whereas for Vrishabha though Rahu has caused Argala, the planets shown in brackets exert counter influence

154. Rasi Strengths

Jaimini always lays great stress on Rasis and their strength. The strength of a Rasi depends upon its own strength *plus* that of the lord. The lord's strength may be assumed to be made up of (*a*) strength due to his distance from the first point of the sign, (*b*) strength derived by his position in Swakshetra, Uchcha, Neecha, etc. (art. 63) and (*c*) a certain disposition from Atmakaraka. A Rasi's own strength is due to (*a*) its association with a planet or planets, (*b*) its being Sthira, Chara or Dwiswabhava, and (*c*) its being aspected by or associated with Jupiter, Mercury or its own lord. The net strength of a Rasi is the total of its own strength *plus* that of the lord. A Rasi could gain special strength by its being occupied by Atmakaraka. An improvised method of numerically determining Rasi strength devised by us has been elaborated in article 62.

Example 51

Determine Rasi and Planetary Strengths in Hitler's horoscope according to the improved method.

Planetary Strengths

Planet	*Moolatri-kona Bala*	*Amsa Bala*	*Kendra Bala*	*Total*
Ravi	60·0	7·5	60	127·5
Chandra	15·0	15·0	15	45·0
Kuja	30·0	45·0	60	135·0
Budha	15·0	3·75	60	78·75
Guru	30·0	22·5	15	67·5
Sukra	15·0	60·0	60	135·0
Sani	7·5	30·0	60	97·5

Rasi Strength

Rasi	*Charabala*	*Drukbala*	*Sthirabala*	*Lord*	*Total*
Mesha	15·0	60 + 60	105·0	135·0	375·0 + 60·0*
Vrishabha	30·0	...		135·0	165·0
Mithuna	60·0	60·0	60·0	78·75	258·75
Kataka	15·0	...	60·0	45·0	120·0
Simha	30·0	60 + 60	...	127·5	275·5
Kanya	60·0	60·0	...	75·75	195·75
Thula	15·0		...	135·0	150·0
Vrischika	30·0	60 + 60	...	135·0	285·0
Dhanus	60·0	60 + 60	90·0	67·5	337·5
Makara	15·0	...	...	97·5	112·5
Kumbha	30·0	60 + 60	...	97·5	247·5
Meena	60·0	60 + 60	...	67·5	247·5

*Add 60 to Mesha for Atmakaraka.

155. Dasas and Bhukthies

The various methods of Dasas recommended by Jaimini always refer to Rasis and the most favoured one appears to be Chara Paryaya Dasa. Aries, Taurus, Gemini, Libra, Scorpio and Sagittarius belong to the Savya group of signs and the rest to the Apasavya group. In calculating any Dasa, two things have to be borne in mind, *viz.*, the order of the Dasas and the span of the Dasa periods as these vary with regard to each horoscope. The span however remains constant in respect of Sthira and Shula Dasas. Taking up Chara Dasa again, the first Dasa invariably starts from Lagna Rasi. The order of succession of Dasas is direct or converse according as the 9th Rasi from Lagna falls in a Savya or Apasavya group. The period of a Rasi is equal to the number of signs intervening between the Rasi and its lord, counted clockwise or anti-clockwise according as the Rasi in question belongs to Savya or Apasavya group. If the lord of the Rasi is Uchha the period is increased by one year ; if the lord is neecha, the period is decreased by one year. In the case of Kambha and Vrischika, as they have two lords each, there is a slight variation in the matter of reckoning their Dasa periods.

The duration of a sub-period or Bhukti is one-twelfth of the duration of a main period or Dasa. If 9th from the Rasi of which sub-periods are required refers to Savya group, the order of succession of the sub-periods is direct, the first being that of the 2nd from the Rasi. If it refers to Apasavya group, the Bhuktis succeeded in the reverse order starting from the 12th from the Rasi concerned.

In Sthira Dasa scheme, a Chara, a Sthira and a Dwiswabhava Rasi, gets 7, 8 and 9 years respectively as its span. The Dasa starts from the sign occupied by Brahma and the other Dasas succeed in the direct order.

The Thrikona Dasa starts from the strongest Rasi out of Lagna, 5th and 9th, and other Dasas run in the direct or converse order according as the starting Rasi refers to Savya or Apasavya group. The Dasa span of a Rasi is the same as in the case of Chara Dasa. Refer for further details to article 93.

In the case of Varnada Dasa, it starts from Lagna and runs in the direct order if the Lagna is odd. If the Lagna is even, the Dasa starts from the 12th and runs in the reverse order. The span of a Dasa is the distance measured in terms of signs from Lagna to the Varnada concerned. Brahma Dasa starts from Brahma Rasi and runs in the direct order, or starts from the 7th from Brahma and runs in the reverse order, according as Lagna is odd or even. The span of a Dasa is the distance from the Rasi concerned to the Rasi occupied by the lord of the 6th from the Rasi in question. The span of the Rasi Dasa in Yogardha Dasa is the mean of its Sthira and Chara Dasa periods. The order is direct or otherwise according as the Rasi of the first Dasa (which will be Lagna or the 7th whichever is stronger), is odd or even. Niryana Shula Dasa is of considerable importance. It is employed for determining the life-terms of the native and his relatives.

Example 52

Find (1) Chara Dasa, (2) Sthira Dasa, (3) Thrikona Dasa, (4) Brahma Dasa, (5) Varnada Dasa and (6) Niryana Shula Dasa, in Hitler's horoscope.

Table of Rasi Dasas in Hitler's Chart

Chart Dasa

Thula	...	6 years
*Vrischika	...	5 ,,

---

* Among the co-lords, Kuja and Ketu, the former alone should be considered being associated with more planets (*vide* Art. 86).

Dhanus	...	12 years
Makara	...	6 "
*Kumbha	...	8 "
Meena	...	36 "
Mesha	...	12 "
Vrishabha	...	11 "
Mithuna	....	10 "
Kataka	...	7 "
Simha	...	5 "
Kanya	...	5 "

Sthira Dasa

Since Sthira Dasa commences from the Rasi where Brahma is posited, the order of different Rasi Dasas will proceed as follows (*vide* Article 91):

1st Dasa	Dhanus	9 years
2nd "	Makara	7 "
3rd "	Kumbha	8 "
4th "	Meena	9 "
5th "	Mesha	7 "
6th "	Vrishabha	8 "
7th "	Mithuna	9 "
8th "	Kátaka	7 "
9th "	Simha	8 "
10th "	Kanya	9 "
11th "	Thula	7 "
12th "	Vrischika	8 "
		96 years

* Lords of Kumbha, Rahu and Sani, are placed in different sign and hence we have to apply art. 86. Both are unassociated. But Rahu is in a more powerful Rasi and also gives more year as the Dasa span.

Thrikona Dasa (Art. 93) :

The 9th house is the strongest out of the three Thrikonas in view of the fact that it happens to be a Dwiswabhava Rasi and also has a plane in it. Since Mithuna falls in the Savya group, the succession of Dasas proceed in the direct order as shown below :—

1st Dasa		Mithuna	10 years
2nd	"	Thula	6 "
3rd	"	Kumbha	8 "
4th	"	Kataka	7 "
5th	"	Vrischika	5 "
6th	"	Meena	3 "
7th	"	Simha	5 "
8th	"	Dhanus	12 "
9th	"	Mesha	12 "
10th	"	Kanya	5 "
11th	"	Makara	6 "
12th	"	Vrishabha	11 "

Brahma Dasa (Art. 96) :

The Lagna is odd and hence the Dasa commences from Brahma Rasi and the order of succession is direct. The span of life contributed by each Rasi beginning from Dhanus is given below :—

Dhanus	4 years
Makara	— 3 "
Kumbha	— 10 "
Meena	— 1 "
Mesha	— 12 "
Vrishabha	— 11 "
Mithuna	— 10 "
Kataka	— 5 "
Simha	— 11 "

Kanya	— 10 years
Thula	— 2 "
Vrischika	— 5 "

Niryana Shula Dasa (Art. 98) :

In Hitler's horoscope, the Lagna being odd, the Dasa starts from Lagna, *viz.*, Thula followed by Vrischika, Dhanus, Makara.................. ......and Kanya each contributing 9 years.

Varnada Dasa (Art. 95) :

Lagna is odd and the Dasa commences from Lagna, *viz.*, Thula.

Janma Lagna is Thula.

Varnada Lagna is Kataka.

Counting in the direct order from Thula to Kataka, we get 10 as the span of the 1st Varnada Dasa. To find out the 2nd Varnada Dasa first we have to fix up the Varnada Lagna for the 2nd house, *viz.*, Vrischika as per rules given in Article 23.

The 2nd Rasi from Lagna = Vrischika (even).

The 2nd from Hora Lagna = Mithuna (odd).

$\therefore a = 5.$

$b = 3.$

$c = 2.$

Since the 2nd from Lagna is an even sign, the 2nd (*c*) from Meena, *viz.*, Kumbha becomes the Varnada of the 2nd Rasi. Now for the span of the 2nd Varnada Dasa, count from Thula to Kumbha which gives 5 years. In a like manner, the duration of the rest of the Varnada Rasis have to be found out.

156. Longevity

Longevity has to be ascertained from (*a*) lords of Lagna and 8th, (*b*) Lagna and Moon and (*c*) Lagna and

Hora Lagna. Alpayu, Madhyayu and Poornayu are revealed by a certain disposition of these six factors in movable, fixed and common signs. Where the three sets of factors reveal three different terms, prefer the one indicated by Lagna and Hora Lagna. In such a case, if the Moon is in Lagna or 7th, consider the term given by (*b*); otherwise give preference to the majority indications. According to another method (Art. 111) the longevity would be Alpa, Madhya or Poorna according as the planet (the stronger of the lords of 8th from Lagna and the 8th from 7th) is in Kendra, Panapara or Apoklima. In the third method suggested in Art. 112 the planet considered is the stronger of the lords of the 8th and 2nd from Atmakaraka. By a judicious consideration of the *pros* and *cons* the term of life of an individual should be carefully fixed. A particular term of life is capable of being replaced by a higher or shorter term and conditions for such Kaksha Vriddhi and Kaksha Hrasa have been dealt with in Art. 114 *et seq*.

Example 53

Find the term of life in Hitler's horoscope.

Term of Life (Art. 104)

(A) The three sets to be considered for deciding whether Hitler's horoscope falls under Poornayu, Madhyayu or Alpayu are: (*a*) Sukra (lord of Lagna and 8th), (*b*) Thula and Chandra (Lagna and the Moon) and (*c*) Thula and Vrishabha (Lagna and Hora Lagna).

	Art. 83 Alpa	Art. 84 Madhya	Art. 85 Poorna
Lord of Lagna—Venus Lord of 8th—Venus	X	X	Poorna
Lagna—Thula Moona—Dhanus	Alpa	X	X
Lagna—Thula Hora—Vrishabha	X	Madhya	X

The above table shows the three sets reveal three different terms. Hence as per Article 108, we have to choose the term shown by "Lagna and Hora Lagna", *viz.*, Madhyayu ; in other words as per method "A" the term is Middle Life.

Method B (Art. 111)

Lord of 8th from Lagna is Venus and the 8th from 7th is owned by Mars. In this case, the question of the stronger among these two does not arise at all. Since both Venus and Mars happen to be in Kendra, the term of life should be Poorna.

Method C (Art. 112)

The planets involved are again Mars and Venus. Therefore the third method confirms B.

Thus we have A indicating Madhyayu, and B and C indicating Poornayu. Consequently, the chart belongs to the category of Poornayu. The next step in the determination of longevity is to see whether the term of life revealed above is subject to any reduction or otherwise, *i.e.*, to Kaksha Hrasa or Kaksha Vriddhi (Art. 114).

Kaksha Vriddhi

Benefics in Thrikona from 7th	=	1
Benefics in Thrikona from Atmakaraka	=	1
		2 units

Kaksha Hrasa

8th lord becomes Atmakaraka	=	1
8th lord from 7th joins Atmakaraka	=	1
Malefic Rahu in Thrikona	=	1
,, from 7th from Atmakaraka	=	1
		4 units

Though Poornayu is shown in the first analysis, the factors for Kaksha Hrasa are more than those for Kaksha Vriddhi. Consequently, the chart belongs to the category of Madhyayu. It must be noted that there is increase of one Rasi Dasa, by the position of the Full Moon in trine to Atmakaraka (*vide* Art. 118).

157. Period of Death

Disposition of Rahu, Ketu or Saturn in the 7th from Lagna or Atmakaraka determines when death takes place in the 1st, 2nd or 3rd part of the term of Ayus earned by the native. Death generally happens in Rasis (*a*) which are trine to 8th, (*b*) subjected to Papakarthari Yoga, (*c*) having malefics in the 8th and 12th, (*d*) in the 8th and 12th Rasi if they have no aspects of planets other than Moon and Venus, (*e*) in the Rasis of Rudra and Maheswara. The Rasi chosen must be consistent with with the fact of its Dasa running within the prescribed term of Ayus.

Example 54

Find the maraka period in the horoscope of Hitler.

Looking into the possible Rasis capable of killing the native, we find the following ones qualified :—

Art. 121 (*b*) Vrishabha, Kanya and Makara.

(*f*) Vrishabha is hemmed in between malefics and hence a death-inflicting Rasi.

(*g*) The 8th and 12th Rasis are Vrishabha and Kanya respectively. Out of these two, Kanya Rasi Dasa is ruled out as it falls in the Poornayu Section irrespective of the Dasa chosen. The other Rasi, *viz*., Vrishabha also gets disqualified due to the aspect of Sani on it.

(*h*) Saturn is in the 8th from the Moon and so there is a possibility of death happening one Rasi earlier.

(*i*) Vrischika also is qualified.

(*j*) Mesha—due to the location of Maheswara.

(*k*) Mesha—due to the location of Rudra.

(*m*) The lords of 3, 6, 8 and 12 from Atmakaraka are Mercury, Mars and Jupiter. Mars being stronger than the other two (Art. 59) the Rasi held by him namely Mesha is qualified.

Thus from the foregoing it will be seen that the stress on Mesha is indeed very heavy followed next by Vrishabha. Before deciding finally Mesha as the death-inflicting Rasi, we shall see what Art. 147 has to say in the matter. Here the reference is to Sula Dasa and the Thrikona Rasis from the stronger of the Lagna and the 7th are the sensitive signs. In the present case undoubtedly the 7th (Mesha) is not only stronger than Lagna but strongest among its trines also. Evidently we should expect the native's death during the Dasa period of Mesha Rasi. According to Niryana Sula Dasa, the period of Mesha Rasi commences with Hitler's 55th year and will continue till his 64th year.

Next we shall see the most critical period during these nine years. It is said that the death can be brought about in the sub-Dasa of the strongest of the lords of the 6th, 2nd and 12th from Atmakaraka (*Venus*), or the Rasi occupied by Rudra (*Mesha*) or in the minor period of the Navamsa Rasi held by the lord of the 6th from Maraka Rasi (*Vrishabha*—the 6th lord from Mesha, Mercury is in Vrishabha Navamsa). So the sub-periods of Mesha and Vrishabha are highly critical and Hitler died in his 56th year during the minor period of Vrishabha.

158. Judging a Horoscope

The nature of the Karakamsa, Navamsa and Varnada Lagna lords determines the personal appearance of the person, while his character and mind are largely revealed by planetary dispositions from Karakamsa. Combinations for wealth are generally referred to Arudha Lagna and the best combination for wealth is an aspect or association between the Atmakaraka and the 2nd lord from him.

Different planets rising in or aspecting Karakamsa indicate one's pre-disposition towards different troubles and dangers. For instance, Karakamsa being Aries suggests fear from cats and rats. When Karakamsa is Sagittarius, there will be accidents from conveyances, falls from high places, etc. Mars, Rahu and Ketu in different positions from Karakamsa indicate different diseases one is likely to suffer from.

Educational prospects are also analysed with reference to planetary dispositions from Karakamsa. Upapada is employed for ascertaining details about brothers and sisters. These are enumerated in Article 132, and combinations indicating death of brothers and sisters. Upapada is the starting point for knowing the affairs of marriage. Benefics and malefics in the 2nd and 7th from Upapada give a clue to understand the general disposition of the 7th house. Widowhood is caused by the disposition of the Sun in a Thrikona from Lagna in the Navamsa, as also by Ketu and Mars occupying the 8th from Hora Lagna. The 5th and 11th houses from Upapada describe the framework of children. Then we have combinations for childlessness, barenness, etc.

From the point of view of determining profession, Jaimini's method is really unique. Here is wide scope for research and investigation. The main considerations in determining the avocations or nature of livelihood are the position of Karakamsa and the planetary dispositions in certain houses from it.

The nature of death is generally revealed by the 3rd house from Lagna or Atmakaraka. Different planets in the 3rd house denote death by different causes. Good planets bring about a peaceful end while evil ones bring a violent death. Articles 141 and 142 refer to miscellaneous combinations denoting charities, devotion, moksha, sympathy, etc.

Example 55

Find the nature of Hitler's death.

According to Jaimini, the nature of one's death has to be decided from the 3rd house from Lagna or from the Atmakaraka. Malefics in the 3rd denote violent end and benefics a peaceful one. Here Rahu is in the 3rd from Atmakaraka and from Lagna the Moon, Jupiter and Ketu. Between Atmakaraka and Lagna if we choose the stronger the former appears to be more powerful in view of the fact that he is associated with three planets whereas Lagna is neither associated with nor aspected by any planet. So Rahu in the 3rd (poison) is the chief indicator though his violent nature is tempered by the aspects of Moon and Jupiter.

159. Timing Events

All important events can be predicted by the Chara Dasa method, while for all events pertaining to death, Sthira and Niryana Sula Dasa may be employed with advantage. Generally, a Rasi gives beneficial results during its Dasa if it is powerful and does not have malefics disposed on either side or in the 8th and 12th. The nature of the results produced by a Rasi Dasa will pertain to the events of the Bhava which it happens to represent from

Lagna or Atmakaraka or even Karakamsa. Death of father can be predicted in the Dasas of Sthira Rasis according to Chara Dasa (Article 145) or in Sthira Rasis according to Niryana Sula Dasa. Similarly, with the aid of these two Dasas can be ascertained the probable periods of death of mother, brothers, children, etc. Even the native's own death can be anticipated on the basis suggested in Article 147.

160. Yogas

A powerful Raja Yoga can be said to exist when Janma Lagna, Hora Lagna and Ghatika Lagna are all simultaneously aspected by a planet. The intensity of the Yoga is lessened if all the three are not aspected. A number of other Raja Yogas indicating rank, position and fame are given. Article 141 describes Arishta Yogas which comprehend a species of misfortunes ranging from diabolical propensities like setting fire to others' houses, to imprisonment and illegal sexual gratifications.

Before leaving Hitler's chart, it is essential that we should look into some of the important features of his horoscope as revealed by the Jaimini System. Looking into his personality, the Karakamsa disposition reflects to a great extent his physical appearance, mental characteristics, etc. Mars when associated with Karakamsa alone is capable of producing a good soldier. Mars–Venus conjunction in Karakamsa raised him from the position of a soldier to that of a ruler and commander. But Ketu's presence in Karakamsa is not desirable. Often the means employed will be questionable—attended with fraud and deceit. Malefics in the 3rd from 1st lord and 7th (Rahu) also is said to make one a Commander. The following are some of the outstanding Raja Yogas which have contributed to his greatness and power :—

Four planets in the 7th from Janma Lagna and Drekkana Lagna, three in Navamsa Lagna and two in the 7th from Navamsa Lagna. So, out of the six factors, four have been fulfilled. Though technically a single planet alone is required (*vide* Raja Yoga 2) we have here four planets thus giving rise to a very powerful Raja Yoga. Added to that, the Yoga gets considerable strength because of the fact that it is generated by the same planets viewed either from Janma Lagna, Drekkana Lagna or Navamsa Lagna.

Another powerful Raja Yoga is caused by the aspects received by the Janma Lagna and Ghatika Lagna and Hora Lagna from Saturn and Mars, Venus and the Moon respectively.

When Mars, Venus and Ketu are in mutual aspects, a Raja Yoga is said to arise. In this chart, though they are not exactly in mutual aspect, there is mutual conjunction.

The conjunction of Atmakaraka with the exalted Sun is itself a Raja Yoga and the most noteworthy factor is that all these Raja Yogas have reference to Mesha Rasi : or in other words Mesha Rasi has become the pivot of Hitler's horoscope. The influences that have been focussed therein are indeed strong. Over and above all these, Mesha has scored 437 points in Rasi Bala. And in his 41st year the Chara Dasa of Mesha Rasi commenced. We have said earlier that the Chara Dasa system is the favourite of Jaimini for timing the events in one's career. It ruled for 12 years and it was during this period that Hitler rose to power and Germany undid the wrongs done to her in the I World War.

THE END

An Index of Technical Terms

Adhana	....	Conception
Adhana Lagna	...	Conception Ascendant
Anhyaya	...	Chapter
Alpayu	...	Short life
Amsa	...	Longitude, planetary—
Amsa Bala	...	Strength due to longitude
Amatyakaraka	....	The lord next in importance to the prime lord
Apasavya	...	Sinistral or anti-clockwise
Apoklima	...	3rd, 6th, 9th and 12th signs
Argala	...	Agency, an obstructing or augmenting—
Argala Chakra	...	Diagrammatic representation of Argalas
Arishta Yogas	...	Unfortunate combinations
Arudha	...	The sign which is as distant from the lord as the lord is from the house concerned
Arudha Lagna	...	The sign as apart from the lord of Lagna as the lord is from Lagna
Ashtottari	....	A system of direction
Atmakaraka	...	The principle or main lord
Ayurdaya	...	Longevity
Bahya Rasi	..	The sign which is as apart from Dwara Rasi as the latter is from Ascendant

Bhavas	... Houses
Bhoga Rasi	... Another name for Bahya Rasi
Bhava Lagna	... A certain kind of Ascendant
Bhratru	... Brother
Bhukti	... Sub-period
Brahma	... A distinction conferred on a planet by certain horoscopic dispositions
Brahma Dasa	... A method of timing events
Brahma Rasi	... Sign occupied by Brahma
Budha	... Mercury
Chakra Dasa	... A method of timing events
Chandra	.... Moon
Chara Bala	... Strength due to the nature—cardinal, etc., of the sign.
Chara Dasa	... A method of direction
Chara Rasi	... Movable sign
Dara	... Wife or husband
Darakaraka	... Lord or indicator of wife or husband
Dasa	... Direction or period ruled by signs
Deerghayu	.... Long life
Deha	... Ascendant or Sun
Dhanurvidyu	.... Science of archery
Dhanus	... Sagittarius
Drekkana	... Decanate
Drig Dasa	... A method of timing events
Druk Bala	... Aspect strength
Durga	... The Principal Destructive Cosmic Force
Dushta Marana	... Violent death

Dwara Rasi	The sign under consideration
Dwiswabhava Rasis	Common signs
Ganapathi	An Aspect of Cosmic Force invoked at the beginning of every venture
Ghatika	24 minutes in time
Ghatika Lagna	A certain kind of Ascendant
Gnathi	Relatives and cousins
Gochara	Planetary transits
Gouri	Consort of Siva
Gulika	A tertiary planet
Guru	Jupiter
Hora	A unit of time-measure equal to I hour
Hora Lagna	A certain kind of Ascendant
Hora Sastra	Science of Time or Astrology
Hrasa	Reduction
Jaimini	A great Indian Sage
Jaghanam	Shanks
Janma Lagna	Ascendant
Jataka	Horoscope
Kaksha	A term or division
Kaksha Hrasa	Decrease of a term of life
Kaksha Vriddhi	Increase of a term of life
Kalatrakaraka	Significator of wife
Kanya	Virgo
Karaka	Significator
Karakamsa	The sign occupied by the prime lord in Navamsa
Kataka	Cancer
Kendra	Quadrant

Kendra Bala ... Strength due to quadrangular position from prime lord
Kendra Dasa ... A method of timing events
Ketu ... Cauda or Dragon's Tail
Kuja ... Mars
Kumbha ... Aquarius

Lagna Rasi ... Ascendant sign
Lagnarudha ... *see* Arudha Lagna
Lakshmi ... Goddess of Wealth

Madhyayu ... Middle Life
Maharshi ... A great seer or sage
Maheswara ... A special distinction conferred on a planet
Makara ... Capricorn
Mandi ... A tertiary planet
Mandooka Dasa ... A method of timing events
Mantravadi ... Wizard
Manushya Jataka ... A Treatise on Horoscopy
Maraka ... Death-inflicting
Maraka Dasa ... The period of death
Maraka Rasi ... Death-inflicting sign
Matru ... Mother
Meena ... Pisces
Mesha ... Aries
Mithra Kshethra ... Friendly sign
Mithuna ... Gemini
Moolatrikona Bala ... Strength due to location or residence

Naisargika Karakas ... Natural significators
Nakshatra Dasa ... A method of timing events
Navamsa ... Ninth devision of a sign

Navamsa Dasa	... A method of timing events
Neecha	.... Debilitation
Neelakanta	... A Commentator
Niryana Shula Dasa	... A method of timing death
Nisheka	... Consummation of marriage
Nisheka Lagna	... Ascendant at consummation
Ojapada	... Odd group
Pada Lagna	... Another name for Arudha Lagna
Paka Rasi	... Another name for Dwara Rasi
Panapara	... 2nd, 5th, 8th and 11th signs
Papargala	... A malefic agency
Parasari	... Parasara's method
Peenasa Roga	... Nasal disease
Pitrukaraka	... Significator of father
Pranapada	... A cestain sensitive point
Prasna Lagna	... Ascendant at question time
Premanidhi	... A Commentator
Prishta	... Buttocks
Purnayu	... Long life
Putra	... Son
Rahu	... Caput or Dragon's Head
Raja Yogas	... Combinations leading to power and fame
Rakta Suvarna	... Reddish yellow
Rasi Bala	... Strength of signs
Rasi Dasa	... Ruling period of a sign
Rasi Hrasa	... Reduction or loss of a sign
Rasi Vriddhi	... Increase or gain of a sign
Ravi	... Sun
Rudra	... A special distinction conferred on a planet

Samakshetra	...	Neutral sign
Samarsingh	....	An Author of a Treatise on Prenatal Astrology
Samapada	...	Even group
Sambasiva	...	Another name for Siva
Sani	...	Saturn
Sanyasa Yogas	...	Combinations for asceticism
Sapta Vargas	..	Seven kinds of sign-divisions
Savya	...	Clockwise
Shadbalas	...	Six sources of strength
Shadvargas	...	Six kinds of sign-divisions
Shanmukha	...	The six-faced son of Siva
Shashtiamsas	...	Units of strength
Simha	...	Leo
Siva	...	One of the Hindu trinity typifying the destructive aspect of Cosmos
Sthira Bala	...	Strength due to the presence of one or more planets in a sign
Sthira Rasi	...	Fixed sign
Subha Marana	....	Natural death
Subhargala	...	Benefic augmenting agency
Sukra	...	Venus
Sula Dasa	...	A method of timing events
Sutras	....	Aphorisms
Swakshetra	...	Own house
Thrikona Dasa	...	A method of timing events
Thula	....	Libra
Uccha	...	Exaltation
Udu Dasa	...	A method of timing events
Upapada	...	The sign as apart from 12th lord as the latter is from 12th

Vahana Yogas	...	Combinations for possessing conveyances
Varnada Dasa	...	A method of timing events
Varnada Lagna	...	A certain kind of Ascendant
Vimshottari	...	A system of directions
Vishamapada	...	Odd group
Vishnu	...	The protective aspect of Hindu Trinity
Vriddhi	...	Increase
Vriddha Yavana	...	An ancient writer on Astrology
Vrischika	...	Scorpio
Vrishabha	....	Taurus
Yogakaraka	...	A planet conferring power, fame, etc.
Yogardha Dasa	....	A method of timing events
Yogas	...	Certain planetary combinations

17.	Varshaphal	15-00
18.	Bhavartha Ratnakara	20-00
19.	A Mannual of Hindu Astrology	15-00
20.	Three Hundred Important Combinations	30-00
21.	Prasna Tantra	22-50
22.	Hindu Astrology and the West	30-00
23.	My Experiments with Astrhology (1926 -1936)	25-00
24.	B. V. Raman : The man and His Mission (Felicitation Volume) Ed : S. V. Jayasheela Rao	75-00
25.	A Study in Astrological Occultism — Bepin Behari	30-00
26.	Palmistry-Marriage and Family Welfare — M. Katakkar	15-00
27.	A Treatise on Palmistry — "	150-00
28.	Unfolding Your Destiny — Keta Meera Sahebu	15-00

Books on Astrology

by Suryanarain Rao

1.	Stri Jataka	12–50
2.	Jaiminisutras	20–00
3.	Compendium of Astrology	10–00
4.	Brihat Jataka	65–00

by Dr. B. V. Raman

1.	Graha and Bhava Balas	10–00
2.	Muhurtha or Electional Astrology	20–00
3.	Planetary Influences on Human Affairs	15–00
4.	Ayurveda	3–00
5.	Astrology for Beginners	8–00
6.	Ashtakavarga System of Prediction	20–00
7.	Prasna Marga (Vol. I)	60–00
8.	Prasna Marga (Vol. II)	45–00
9.	Ninety Years Ephemeris of Planetary Positions (1891 to 1980)	30–00
10.	Raman's 20 Years Ephemeris (1981 to 2000 A.D.)	15–00
11.	How to Judge a Horoscope (Vol. I)	40–00
12.	How to Judge a Horoscope (Vol. II)	50–00
13.	Notable Horoscopes	40–00
14.	A Catechism of Astrology (Vol. I)	9–00
15.	A Catechism of Astrology (Vol. II)	9–00
16.	Hindu Predictive Astrology	40–00